MURDER IN MIND

J.D. Pearson

First published 2025
by Rowanvale Books Ltd
The Gate
Keppoch Street
Roath
Cardiff
CF24 3JW
www.rowanvalebooks.com

A CIP catalogue record for this book is available from the British Library.
Paperback ISBN: 978-1-83584-127-3
eBook ISBN: 978-1-83584-128-0

I would very much like to thank the following people who helped with this book.

Paula Shettlesworth—you not only gave me great encouragement, but you also helped with the story itself. The back story, which was very personal to you and hard to talk about, was amazing and a big part of the main character and her actions. Thank you so much—you're an amazing person.

Ash Shuttlewood—you came up with the brilliant title of the book, and I'd also like to thank you for your encouragement along the way.

I would also like to thank my beta readers Jamie, Sam, Tracy, June, and Sharron for taking the time to read the book and give feedback.

CHAPTER ONE

Gina was enjoying the silence around her as she finished another page of her colouring book, when suddenly Toby barked.

"Toby! You made me jump!" she said.

He leapt out of his bed and onto the sofa, putting his head through the gap in the curtains. Gina put down the book and went to the window.

"What is it, boy?" She looked up and down the village but couldn't see anything. It was quite dark but just light enough to see if anyone was lurking around outside. Toby had reduced his barking to a growl, and it was then Gina heard sirens getting closer. She saw an ambulance and two police cars pull up to the house opposite.

She went to the front door, shutting Toby in the living room. Dressed in her white shirt and yellow shorts, she stood in the now open doorway for a minute before walking to the middle of the road to get a better look.

Her mouth fell open as she saw a woman's body lying motionless on the grass next to the driveway of the large Victorian-style house opposite her own two-bedroom property. She tried to move closer and saw three paramedics attending to the lady, before a policeman ushered her away. Gina recognized the woman as Annie Spencer, the house's occupant. She stood by her gate, feeling a little frustrated that a big bush was blocking her view. All Gina could see was the driveway and the front door. As she watched, two police officers forced the front door open and entered while another two stayed outside.

A large woman came out of the house next door to Gina and went across the road, but the policeman ushered her back. Gina shook her head as the woman— her neighbour, Tracy—argued with them. Eventually, Tracy came back towards her.

"What did you do to Annie? Push her out the window?"

Gina looked up. The bedroom window of Annie's house was wide open. "No, I didn't."

"You were seen coming out of her house this afternoon."

"You think *I* had something to do with this, Tracy?"

"What were you doing in there? We all heard the blazing row you had with her a couple of weeks ago. I think the police would be interested in that information."

Tracy walked away.

Gina swallowed. A forensics van had pulled up, and a man and a woman got out, wearing white overalls. They took a black leather bag out of the back and went into the house.

Gina was joined by her other neighbour, Sue, who looked very concerned.

"Alright, Sue?"

"What happened?" Sue said.

"I've no idea. Looks like Annie's had an accident."

Gina surveyed the crowd. Tracy and three other women were talking among themselves and kept looking at her.

"They think I had something to do with it," she said.

"It's just Tracy," said Sue. "You know what she's like."

The sound of a siren pulled Gina's attention: the ambulance lights flashed blue, and it shot out of the driveway and disappeared up the road, out of the village.

Gina looked up at the window, where the forensics officer was dusting the windowpanes and handle. She felt like taking some more anxiety tablets, but she had already taken her full dose for the day, so she took deep breaths to try to calm herself down. Watching the crowd closely, she could see they were all muttering to each other. Tracy and the other ladies were talking to a policewoman, huddled together, gesturing in Gina's direction. She tried to ignore them, but she couldn't help staring; she knew they were talking about her. Tracy was doing most of the talking as the police officer wrote in her notebook, sometimes glancing in her direction.

Gina looked at the open window again. The two forensic officers seemed to be in deep discussion. As the police officer peered at her again, she popped the hip of her yellow shorts and flicked her hair. She hadn't done anything wrong. Sure, she had been at Annie's that afternoon, but she hadn't pushed her out of the window. How could they think she'd done it if they'd seen her leave?

Tracy called out to Sue and beckoned her over. Gina stood alone; her hands were clammy and her mouth felt like she'd been in a hot desert for days. She watched everyone huddled in their groups. They were chatting, and some glared in her direction.

They all think I did it, she thought. She could hear their thoughts and whispers: *Murderer! She killed Annie. She KILLED her!*

Gina had seen enough. She went back inside and downed a full pint of water, then poured herself a glass of wine and sat down in her black chair, reclining it to stretch her legs. Toby jumped up and lay beside her. He started snoring slightly. Gina tried to relax and block out the accusing voices of her neighbours. She tapped her fingers on the side of the chair, taking deep breaths to keep herself calm.

There was a sudden knock at the door, and she jumped. Toby barked and leapt off the chair. She picked him up and held him under her arm as she opened the door. Standing there was a tall man in a navy suit with straight, jet-black hair that was slicked back.

"Good evening. I'm DS Carter. I'm looking for Mrs Wilkinson."

"That's me. But it's *Miss* Wilkinson."

"Apologies. I'm sorry to disturb you, but we need to talk to you about Mrs Spencer."

Gina stared at his identity card, then opened the door wider, inviting him in—but he didn't move.

"We would like you to accompany us to the station."

Gina's heart rate went up, her chest tightening. "What for? I don't know what happened. What's everyone been saying?"

"Calm down. You're not being arrested; you're just helping with our enquiries. We have received information that could help us with our investigation." He had a kind voice, which calmed her nerves. "We will bring you back home, assuming we're satisfied with what you tell us."

Gina looked at her phone. It was nearing 10 p.m. "It's late. I'll be getting ready for bed soon. I'll come first thing in the morning."

The detective put his hand on the door, stopping it from shutting. "It's best if we do this now. I'm sorry it's late, but it's important. We'll bring you home, I promise."

She scowled, then sighed. "I need to get Toby's lead."

"I'm afraid you can't bring the dog," Carter said.

Ignoring him, Gina went to get Toby's lead from the kitchen cupboard.

"He's an assistance dog," she said.

Carter sighed as he saw the yellow band attached to the lead with "ASSISTANCE DOG" across it. "Okay, you can bring him, but he's not allowed in the interview room."

"Where I go, Toby goes," she said, not moving.

Carter rolled his eyes. "Chief Inspector won't be happy, but alright."

A uniformed policewoman held Gina's arm and led her towards the police car. She kept her head down, buried in Toby's neck, as she felt all eyes burning on her. A hand touched her shoulder.

"Try not to worry. You've done nothing wrong. I'm here for you, love."

Sue's words sounded pleasant, but Gina didn't feel much better; she still heard whispers from the other neighbours.

She got in the back of the car with the policewoman, Toby on her lap. *How did I get into this situation?* The question ripped through her mind as the car sped out of the village.

CHAPTER TWO

The journey to the station was quiet, and Gina kept her head down, taking deep breaths and trying to control how she was feeling. She wanted to wake up, for all this to be a nightmare. She stroked Toby gently and prayed they would take her home that evening. The thought of being in a cell all night was unbearable, and she worried about poor Toby. He was such a small dog, so fluffy and cute. Suddenly she felt very sick as the awful thought hit her that if she was in a cell, they would put Toby in a separate cage; but the feeling passed as it occurred to her that because Toby couldn't be away from her due to her mental health, they would bring her home. Besides, she'd done nothing wrong—she was being dragged down the station because of her neighbours. Gina glanced up at the officer sitting next to her, but the woman just stared out of the window.

At the station, Gina was led to a small room with Toby in her arms. There were no windows—just a table and three chairs. She wasn't fingerprinted, which was a relief, but as she waited, her palpitations got worse. Her fingers were clammy. She turned to the policewoman standing by the door. "Why am I here?"

The policewoman just stood there.

Gina again buried her head in Toby's neck. She felt tired and drained; she should be curled up at home with Toby, not sitting in a small, dingy room at the police station. She couldn't believe this was real. Even Toby, looking around anxiously, seemed confused about what was happening.

The door opened, and Detective Carter walked in. He was followed by another man, shorter with grey hair and a beard.

"I'm DS Carter," he said, introducing himself again. "This is Detective Chief Inspector Kene."

Gina looked at her phone. It was approaching 11 p.m. "Would you mind telling me why I've been brought here at this time of night?"

"Yes, of course, Miss Wilkinson. You're not under arrest; we just need to ask you a few questions about Mrs Spencer."

"Why couldn't you ask me at home? And why couldn't this wait till the morning?" Gina raised her voice; she was struggling to control herself.

"We thought it would be better if we asked here, while it was still fresh," Carter said. "Please try to keep calm."

"How is Annie?" Gina asked. Sweat rolled down her forehead.

"She's in critical condition."

"I still can't understand why this couldn't wait till tomorrow. I could've come here then."

"Because we wanted to talk to you tonight, Miss Wilkinson," Kene said abruptly. He had a strong Scottish accent. "And the sooner we get on with it, the sooner you can go home. I myself would also like to get home. I've been here for thirteen hours and need to get some sleep. So let's get on with it, shall we?"

The door opened, and a female police officer came in. She strode over to the table, then reached out to Toby, on Gina's lap, and put her hands under his chest.

Toby yelped.

Gina flinched and clutched the little dog as tightly as she could without hurting him. "What are you doing? Leave him alone!" she snapped.

"We can't have dogs in here, Miss Wilkinson," Kene said.

"No! He's an assistance dog! He stays with me—you can't take him." Tears started to roll down Gina's cheeks as the woman tried again to grab Toby. This time she was successful; she seized him in her arms and carried him out of the room, the door banging behind her.

"He'll be perfectly fine," Carter said.

Gina smashed her fist down on the table. "You can't take him from me. Under the Equality Act 2010, assistance dogs are allowed in all public places."

"I don't care, Miss Wilkinson," Kene said, raising his voice. "He is not coming in here. The sooner you answer our questions, the quicker you can have him back and go home."

"Mrs Spencer was discovered lying on her lawn in her front garden," Carter said, clearly eager to get this over with. "The bedroom window was wide open, so it's obvious she either fell out or was pushed out in an altercation with someone."

"What's that got to do with me?" Gina asked, trying to control her tone.

"We spoke to some of the neighbours to find out more about Mrs Spencer—who she was friendly with and if she had any enemies. Your name came up a few times."

Gina looked sharply at Carter. "Oh… So you know I was at her place this afternoon?"

"Yes. What were you doing there?"

"She suffers with back pain, so I gave her a massage to try and help."

Carter nodded. "Your neighbours said they saw you and Mrs Spencer having a heated argument a couple of weeks ago. Is that true, Miss Wilkinson?"

Gina hesitated. "Yes, we had a disagreement. Does that mean I pushed her out of the window?"

"What was the argument about?" Kene said, ignoring her question.

Gina's eyes wandered around the room. The walls were closing in on her; she just wanted to get out of there as soon as she could. Her heart was going to burst through her chest any minute. "She wasn't very happy about my dog, Toby. He kept going on the edge of her driveway when I took him for his walks."

She couldn't stop thinking about Toby. *Where is he? Have they locked him in a cage?*

"Is that it?" Carter said. "Because your neighbours said you were shouting at each other."

Gina's fingers came away wet when she wiped her brow. She slumped over the table and started wheezing.

"Are you alright?" Carter asked.

"Where is Toby?"

"He's being looked after."

"I need water, please," Gina said.

Carter nodded at the policewoman standing by the door, who left the room. Tears rolled down Gina's face. Inspector Kene sighed impatiently.

"The sooner you tell us what you know, the quicker this will be over," Carter said.

A uniformed policeman opened the door and beckoned Carter and Kene over. Gina turned around to look; they were whispering, but she couldn't hear what was being said.

A minute later, they came back and sat down. Gina was desperate to know what had been said, but neither officer revealed anything about the conversation.

The policewoman came in with a cup of water. Gina took a big gulp, spilling some of it down her chin. What if they decided to put her in a cell? Or prison? If Annie died, they could charge her with murder! Would she get to see her beloved Toby again? Her mind was racing so much she felt like it was going to explode. How would she cope without Toby?

"I don't feel well! I need to go home!" she said. "I need my Toby."

"Just a few more minutes." Carter put his hand on her arm to prevent her getting up. "So, when you take your dog for a walk, he goes in Mrs Spencer's garden, and the two of you had a big argument about it—is that right?"

"No! He only went on the edge of her driveway. I pulled him away quickly."

"Your neighbours told us the two of you were yelling at each other and nearly came to blows! It's hardly the sort of thing that would cause such a big scene. Just on the edge of the driveway."

"That's what Annie's like—a moaning old bat. And she did most of the yelling." Gina gulped down the rest of the water.

"I think there's something you're not telling us," Kene said. "There has to be something else. Something that perhaps made you snap tonight and go over there, start another fight, get her upstairs and push her out of the window."

Gina's eyes shot at Kene. The way he spoke to her, like a piece of crap just off the streets... Detective Carter had a soothing, calm voice. She felt he took slight pity on her.

She could hardly control her breathing now, and felt like she was going to pass out. Her vision was starting to blur, and nausea churned in her stomach. She took a deep breath. "I didn't push her out the window! I wasn't over there tonight. I was there this afternoon. If the neighbours saw me go over there or leave, then it proves I wasn't there tonight." Her voice was shaky but stern.

Kene leant forward. "Come on, Miss Wilkinson. Tell us what happened. Make it easy on yourself. Three neighbours did see you leave this afternoon. Maybe you didn't do it then, but you went back tonight and pushed her out of the window, didn't you?"

"I told you, I didn't push her out of any window!" Gina was raising her voice now. Tears streamed down her face.

Carter went to say something, but Kene cut him off. "Then how do you explain what happened tonight? Why the only name mentioned as being involved was yours?"

"Maybe she fell out of the window, or jumped. I don't know—how many more times do I have to say it?"

"Then why did you and Mrs Spencer have such a big row and nearly come to—"

"She went to kick my dog!" Gina yelled, slamming her fist on the table. "Toby went on her driveway, I pulled him off—but she came storming out and kicked at him. I was shocked. I can't remember what was said in the argument, but that's what it was about! Happy now? But I didn't push her out the window! I didn't, I tell you!" She paused and took a deep breath. "When I'd calmed down after the argument, I went to her and apologised. I saw she was in pain with her legs and her back, so I thought I'd offer to massage her to try and help. She refused at first, then she agreed. So I went to her place this afternoon, and then went home after, and that was it."

"Are you in the habit of giving massage services to your neighbours?" Kene said.

"I run a small business from home. I offered it to her as a friendly gesture. I haven't been in the village that long; I don't want to go to war with my neighbours. It took some convincing, but she agreed to let me help her. That's what I did this afternoon. I normally have clients come to my place, but she asked me to do it at her house. You can ask her when she recovers."

"We can't ask her," Carter said. "Mrs Spencer died half an hour ago in hospital."

Gina slumped in her chair. She had no idea where that burst of energy had come from, but hearing those words was like a magical bullet hitting her from nowhere. She couldn't speak; she saw the walls closing right in on her, and she just wanted to sleep and never wake up. Her eyelids drooped as she laid her head in her arms across the table, breathing heavily.

Carter frowned at her, concerned again, and the female officer came over to check on her. "I think she's having a panic attack, sir."

"We'd better get the medic, I suppose." Kene sounded irritated.

As the medic arrived to attend to Gina, Carter left the room; Kene also got up to leave. "We'll be talking to you again, Miss Wilkinson," he said, and marched out of the door.

Gina's vision was blurred, and she was hyperventilating. A mask was clamped over her mouth and nose, and she could barely hear what was going on. She breathed deeply into the mask and felt her heart rate decrease gradually. After a few minutes, the mask came off, and she was given a couple of tissues to wipe the sweat off her face.

Carter came back in as she was dabbing her forehead. "I'll take you home."

Gina was still shaking as she got up, but not as much as before. "What time is it?"

"Nearly midnight," he said.

The female officer came back into the room with Toby, and gave him straight to Gina. Her eyes were prickling as she hugged him tight.

Carter held the back door of his BMW open for Gina. They both stayed silent on the way home, Gina hugging Toby on her lap. She started to feel as if she wanted to vomit but, to her relief, managed to hold it down. The village was quiet and empty as they drove towards her house.

Gina carried Toby in, turned back to Carter and said, "I'll be fine."

Before he could say anything, she shut the door.

She got some water and went upstairs, Toby following her all the way. Her panic attack had all but gone; however, the nausea she had experienced in the car returned. She clenched her stomach, but this time it was no good. Gina ran to the bathroom, just making it to the toilet before she vomited. Weakened and light-headed, her eyes out of focus, she slumped over the toilet bowl.

After about twenty minutes, Gina got up and went to the sink, where she splashed water on her face and used some mouthwash. Pained by her cramping stomach, she crashed out on her bed. Toby jumped up on the bed and nestled himself against her abdomen, and then neither of them moved until the morning.

CHAPTER THREE

Since being interrogated four days ago, Gina had not stepped out of the house; in fact, she'd done nothing but sit around in her dressing gown. The interrogation that night had almost broken her. Sitting in that room had been bad enough, but them taking Toby away during questioning was completely out of order. Toby was Gina's assistance dog, her aid, and they had no right to do what they did. She knew she should make a complaint, but since her interrogation, all the energy had gone from her mind and body. So Gina hid from the world, dosed up on her medication, and put Toby in the garden instead of taking him on his walks. The only person she'd been in contact with was Sue—but when Sue had tried to see her, Gina had told her she needed to be alone for a while and not to worry. Sue asked if they were still going to the village pub on Friday. Gina had forgotten about it, but told Sue she would still go.

So Gina took an extra dose of medication that Thursday night and decided to get back into her routine in the morning. She didn't want to let her friend down; Sue had been there for her during some hard days when Gina had first moved to the village a year ago.

Her alarm went off at 6.55 a.m. Gina put it on snooze, but when it went off again at seven she went downstairs and made a coffee, Toby shadowing her every move. He sat looking at her the whole time she made his breakfast. After she drank her coffee, Gina brushed her teeth, got dressed and brushed Toby. She loved his fluffy, pure-white fur.

Toby jumped with excitement when he saw his harness. It took her about five minutes to put it on ready for his morning walk, as he wouldn't keep still.

It was a nice sunny day, that Friday in June, and after four days of dosing herself up, sometimes taking more than she should, Gina was eager to get outside in the fresh air. She put on Toby's lead and opened the front door. Her eyes squinted in the bright sunshine and it took a few seconds for them to focus.

I guess that's what you get when you lock yourself inside with the curtains closed, said a voice in her head.

Toby charged out of the gate, pulling Gina's arm as she tried to close the door. They turned right, going past Sue's house. While Toby sniffed the bottom of Sue's wall, Gina looked over at the front of Annie's big house. The blue-and-white police tape was still across the entrance to the driveway.

They passed a row of average-sized detached houses similar to her own, each with their own driveway. Greenville was a small, quiet village; Gina glanced at the neat rows of flowers in the gardens and took in the freshly mowed lawns. A few yards further on was the village store. Though there was an out-of-town shopping centre not far from the village, Gina nearly always got her groceries from the village store; she didn't like to go outside the village on her own unless she had to. She passed the Greenville Inn at the end of the road and, after passing a small row of trees, entered the park just on the edge of the village. Toby led Gina around the outside, stopping to sniff every now and then. Two Yorkshire terriers, not on leads, came running up, which always got Gina nervous. They sniffed around, then their owner whistled them back.

Gina and Toby circled the park. It was quiet; just the man with the terriers, and a couple of toddlers on swings being pushed by their mums. The two terriers came running back towards Gina. They sniffed around Toby and he sniffed them back.

Their owner, an old man wearing a cap, came over and bent down to stroke Toby. "He's a lovely little fellow. Is he a Bolognese?"

"Yes, he is," Gina said. "He's my absolute world."

"He's your assistance dog?" the man said, eyeing the yellow band on Toby's lead. "That means you can take him anywhere you want?"

"That's right," Gina said. "I'm glad somebody understands. I get into quite a few arguments when I take him into some places."

"A lot of people don't understand," the man said. "But you stick to your guns, love, and don't let them win. He's your aid, getting you through difficult times."

Gina stared at the man with a surprised look on her face. But he suddenly looked worried, so she smiled at him and said, "Thank you so much. You're spot on."

She said goodbye to the man and made her way back through the village. She wanted to walk down the same side they had come up, but Toby led her to the other side, sniffing along the walls, marking his territory. There were only three houses on this side, four or five bedrooms with large gardens and driveways. They walked past at a slow pace, with Toby continuing to sniff along the way. There was a low sound of classical music and a smell of sausage and bacon, which made Gina a bit hungry.

They carried on and approached the village church. Gravestones, some subsiding in the ground, surrounded the front. Gina had to pull Toby back as he entered the church grounds; the church was the one place she always tried to avoid, despite being asked by the reverend to give it a try, as she could be helped by God in her troubles.

As they approached Annie's, Toby led Gina across the road and back inside her house. She took off his harness, sat down, took out her phone and dialled the police station.

"Hello, Kent Police, Canterbury," said a woman's voice.

"Yes, hello." Gina swallowed, and started to feel knots in her stomach. "My name is Gina Wilkinson. I was brought in on Monday night for questioning, and I had my assistance dog with me, but just before the interview, he was taken away—I want to make a formal complaint against the officers for not allowing me my assistance dog while I was being questioned."

"We don't allow dogs in interview rooms, dear," the woman said.

Gina's anger started to rise. "He's an assistance dog! He's my aid! If I had to use a walking stick, would you make me leave it outside the room?"

"Calm down, Mrs Wilkinson. It's just… Well, a dog is different from a walking aid."

"It's *Miss* Wilkinson, and clearly you need to look up the law on assistance dogs. I still want to make a complaint."

Gina heard the woman typing on her computer. "Who do you want to make a complaint against?"

"Detective Carter, and Kene—an inspector, I think."

The line went silent for a moment. "Right. I'll make sure your complaint is passed on."

***

Later that afternoon, Gina got out of the shower and put on her light-blue dressing gown. Though she was nervous, she was looking forward to her night out with Sue. She'd just taken her anxiety tablets when the doorbell rang—Sue must have come round a bit early. She opened the door and her anxiety went up. Standing there was DS Carter.

"Miss Wilkinson, can I have a minute of your time?"

Gina rolled her eyes but opened the door to let him in. She pointed him towards the living room, where he looked around, his attention settling on the mantel above the fireplace. There was a fairy ornament at each end, a couple of coin boxes and an old photo of a man, a woman and a little girl.

She folded her arms and sighed. "Is there something I can do for you, Detective? I'm getting ready to go out." Her voice was sharp.

"I just came to tell you we've had the results of the post-mortem examination on Mrs Spencer. There's no evidence of foul play. We tested the fingerprints in her house. Yours were found downstairs, but nothing upstairs."

"My prints weren't taken," Gina said. "How were they on your file?"

"It seems you were charged with assault in a fight with another girl when you were eighteen. The charges were dropped—but once your prints are on file, they stay there."

"I'd forgotten about that."

"The inquest has ruled Annie's death a suicide. The post-mortem showed she'd consumed quite a lot of alcohol. So you're no longer under investigation. Not enough evidence."

Gina's sombre expression didn't change. "Well... Thank you for letting me know. Doesn't help that I suffered during and after that interrogation the other night."

"Yes, about that. I understand you made a complaint against myself and the inspector earlier?"

"Yes, I did. You had no right to take my dog away from me."

"I know that now. One of my colleagues looked up assistance dogs, and you were right—under the Equality Act of 2010, I believe?"

"Yes, that's right," Gina said. "I would have expected the police to know that."

"I know, and I sincerely apologise for our mistake. It was actually DI Kene who made the final decision to not have your dog in the interview room."

"Thank you for your apology, Detective. I'll look forward to his."

Carter looked away. "Inspector Kene is old-school. I'm not sure he's ever made an apology to anyone. He's very set in his ways, if you know what I mean?"

Gina nodded. "I know the type. I'll drop the complaint, as long as it doesn't happen again."

"Thank you. It won't happen again," Carter said. "Can we get back to Mrs Spencer?"

Gina looked at her phone. "Alright, but I don't have much time."

"Do you have any idea why Mrs Spencer might have wished to end her life?"

"No. She seemed alright when I saw her that afternoon. You know, Detective, when people are that depressed, they normally keep it bottled up. They don't tell anyone. The ones that do tell others they're going to take their own life don't really mean it. It's just a cry for help. I learned that over the years."

"When you were in institutions?"

Gina's eyes shot at him.

"We did a background check on you," he said.

Gina said nothing, trying to hold it together.

"You were adopted, right?"

"Yes. My mother abandoned me when I was a baby. She just left me in the hospital. I was raised by another couple. They were my real parents."

"Did you ever have contact with her?"

"She wouldn't leave me alone. Thanks to her, I didn't have a proper, happy childhood."

Putting her hands on her hips, she watched Carter look around her room. He seemed to take a great interest in her belongings.

"Very nice," he said, looking at her diamond painting of a small cottage and garden with mountains in the background. It glittered in the sunlight.

"They're my diamond paintings," she said.

He picked up the one she was working on.

"That one's going to be of my Toby when it's finished."

She looked at the time, and sighed when he went to her bookshelf.

"You like to read, I see?"

"Yes. I do cross-stitch as well."

"Plenty to keep you busy at home."

"I don't go out much. I suffer from bad anxiety, and I have autism. That's why I have Toby with me—I take him almost everywhere."

"Almost?" Carter said.

Gina rolled her eyes, irritated that she had to explain everything. "If I'm with someone I'm comfortable with, I might leave him at home on the odd occasion."

Carter nodded. "I understand."

Gina wasn't sure she believed him. "I don't go out on my own. That's why he had to come with me to the station—not that I deserved to get dragged down there so late at night and get shoved in a room with no windows, being accused of murder, then have him taken away!"

Carter just nodded. "So, you have no more information on why—"

"Detective, I don't mean to be rude," Gina said, "but I need to get ready. I have no more information on Annie. So, if there's anything else…?"

"No, that's all. You take care now."

While Gina finished getting ready, putting makeup on in front of her heart-shaped mirror, thoughts of her birth mother kept entering her head. She tried hard to push her out, but Karen was like an annoying song stuck in her mind.

CHAPTER FOUR

1974

Gina sat waiting in her coat and woolly hat. She started crying, clinging to her mum. "I don't want to go with her."

Lynda held Gina tight on her lap. "You'll be fine. She's taking you shopping."

The doorbell rang. A slim, fair-haired woman stood there, puffing on a cigarette. Lynda kissed the top of Gina's head as she set her down gently on her feet, but it wasn't enough to stop her tears.

Karen reached out to grab Gina's hand.

"No! Don't want to!"

"Come on, love," Lynda said. "It's not for long."

Reluctantly, Gina took Karen's hand and they headed out of the door.

Once in the town centre, they met another woman.

"Say hello to your Auntie Carol, Gina," Karen said.

Gina lowered her head and said nothing.

Without hesitation, Karen grabbed Gina's arm and smacked her bottom hard. When she wailed, Karen shook her. "You be polite and say hello to your Aunt Carol!"

"It's alright, sweetie. You're just a bit shy," Carol said.

Gina stopped crying and wiped her eyes. "H... Hello," she mumbled, the word barely coming out.

After what seemed like hours of wandering in and out of shops, Gina started crying again, complaining she was tired. As her wailing grew louder, Karen—who had been trying to ignore her—took her down a quiet alley and smacked the backs of her legs several times.

Gina screamed.

"Carol, can you take her home, please?" Karen stormed off, out of sight.

Carol took Gina by the hand and began to walk back in the direction of Lynda's road.

"Which house is yours, sweetie?"

Gina pointed to a purple door. She recognised the flowers in the front window.

Lynda didn't expect to open the door to someone she'd never met.

"Hi, Lynda. I'm Carol, Karen's sister."

Lynda looked up and down the road, but Karen was nowhere to be seen.

CHAPTER FIVE

The doorbell rang just as Gina finished getting ready, making Toby bark. When she opened the door, Sue was standing there in a long blue dress; Gina suddenly felt underdressed in her white shirt and purple leggings. Sue tensed up as Toby jumped up her leg, so Gina scooped him up in her arms, kissed the top of his head, told him she wouldn't be too long, and followed Sue out of the door.

"Haven't heard much from you lately," Sue said as they walked up towards the village pub.

"Sorry, love. I needed some time to myself." Gina's voice was low and sad. "That night with Annie, then being dragged down the police station, it knocked the stuffing out of me."

Sue put her arm around her.

"It's alright, Sue." Her chest tight, Gina barely got the words out.

Sue pulled Gina into her arms as all the emotion came flooding out and she sobbed hard.

"Get it out," Sue whispered.

They walked into the pub, and Gina went straight to the ladies. She looked at herself in the mirror: her eyes were puffy, and her mascara had run. She splashed water on her face, dabbed herself dry with a paper towel, then applied more mascara and tidied her hair.

She joined Sue at the bar, where she requested a gin and tonic, before going into the garden. It was a pleasant setting; round wooden tables with chairs were placed at one end, a children's play area at the other.

Gina sat next to a pond where lily pads calmly floated in water which glittered in the light of the low sun.

She enjoyed the calmness; it was therapeutic. However, it was soon broken by a little boy of about five who came and stood next to her. She smiled and was about to say hello when a woman came over and dragged him away to the table she was sharing with an older lady. The woman knelt down to the boy's level and shook him, raising her voice about approaching strangers. Gina just watched in disbelief. The boy had only stood near her, and she felt the shaking was unnecessary. The boy started wailing, and the woman told him to shut up.

Gina took a mouthful of her drink as soon as Sue gave it to her.

"That's the woman who was taken away by the police," said the elder of the two women.

Gina glared at them; they turned away sharply.

She told Sue what had happened, and Sue shrugged.

"Does everyone think I pushed Annie out the window?" Gina whispered.

Sue tried to reassure her. "Of course not! Take no notice. People just like to gossip."

"They live in the big house next to the church in the village, don't they?" Gina said, keeping her voice to a whisper.

"Yeah, they're mother and daughter. I've spoken to them a couple of times in church. I've seen them talk with Tracy."

Gina felt a rush of blood and bit her lip. "I might have known Tracy would turn people against me." She took another sip of her drink.

"Like I said, it's only gossip. Tracy's that kind of person, she spreads rumours. There was no evidence you were in Annie's house that night. And I know you would never do anything like that anyway. Tracy's not worth worrying about."

Gina smiled. Sue's kind words were reassuring.

They both finished their drinks, and Sue got up. "Same again?"

"Absolutely. My shout." Gina handed Sue some money.

As the evening wore on, the atmosphere lightened. Both Gina and Sue were giggling like a couple of teenage girls. They were also getting a bit loud, and other people were giving them annoyed looks. But Gina felt completely different than she had earlier when she'd broken down in Sue's arms.

While Sue was getting what would be their last round of drinks before going home, a man came over to Gina. He was chubby in the face, with thin grey hair and a beer belly.

"Hey, Colin, how are you?" Gina said, her words slurring slightly.

"You've had a good evening, then?" Colin said.

"Yeah. I'm here with Sue. We're having a good time." Gina noticed Colin putting his hand around his back and wincing. "You in pain, Colin?"

"It's just me back. It's been giving me a bit of trouble lately."

"It's stress, being married to Tracy." Gina sniggered. "Do you want me to massage it for you?"

"Oh… No thanks."

Gina stood up. "I give good, deep, relaxing massages, Colin—some soothing oil and my magic hands could help your back problem, I reckon."

She sat back down as Sue returned with another drink.

"You two are going to feel it in the morning," Colin said. "I'd get on home if I were you."

"Sue, tell Colin how good my massages are."

"Fantastic!" Sue said. "I would recommend Gina's massages to anyone. I always nearly fall asleep."

"I'll see how I get on." Colin sounded somewhat nervous.

"Well, you know where I am," Gina said. "Right next door."

It was nearly midnight when Gina and Sue staggered home. They linked arms to stop each other falling over, and hugged before they went indoors.

Toby barked and wagged his tail when Gina walked through the door. Not in any condition to give him her usual excited greeting, she slowly bent down to stroke him; then, holding on to the banister, she staggered upstairs. She got on the bed without getting undressed and was out like a light as soon as her head hit the pillow, with Toby taking his position against her chest.

***

The next morning, Gina took her daily tablets—as well as some painkillers—with some strong coffee. Her head felt like someone was trying to hammer their way out from the inside. She let Toby in from the garden, gave him his breakfast and sipped her coffee.

Then she went back upstairs and buried herself under her covers; she wasn't in any mood to take Toby for his morning walk.

She awoke with Toby's frantic barking hammering inside her head, then heard a thump on the door. The thumping continued—but Gina's head was thumping harder, so she just ignored it. Eventually, the noise stopped, and Toby joined Gina on the bed. It was light outside, but she didn't have any motivation to move.

Toby barked again and leapt off the bed, making Gina jump. She looked at her bedside clock and saw it was just gone midday; her head felt better now, so she got out of bed.

She let Toby out in the back garden, then heard someone banging on her front door. Just as she unbolted it and turned the handle, the door burst open. Gina grabbed the banister to stop herself falling over.

"You've got some explaining to do, *bitch*!"

Speechless, all she could do was stare at Tracy Harper.

CHAPTER SIX

"Do come in, Tracy," Gina said as Tracy shoved past her, barging into the house uninvited.

"Had a good time last night?" Tracy said. She got right into Gina's face. Garlic breath mixed with cigarettes made Gina almost gag.

"Oh… Yeah. I think so."

Gina was confused. Why was Tracy looking so red-faced? What could she have done to make her neighbour so mad?

"Don't know what I'm talking about? Then let me remind you. Last night you offered my husband a massage, did you not?" Tracy fixed her eyes on Gina, waiting for a response.

Gina put her hand on the side of her head. "Oh… Yes. He said something about having back trouble, so I offered to massage him to see if I could help. What's wrong with that? It was an innocent offer to help."

"What's wrong with that!?" Tracy said, taking another step closer to her. "So it never crossed your mind to lure my husband in here to lead him to your bedroom?"

Gina chuckled. "I massage quite a few clients, men and women. I just run a small business. Nothing like that goes on here."

"You're lying, bitch! We all know what goes on in this place. We all know what you do."

Gina was finding it very difficult to keep calm. "I'm telling you now—"

"I don't give a fuck what you say!" Tracy yelled. "This was a respectable village, then you came along. The whole village knows what you get up to. If you think we're going to let you tarnish the good reputation of this community, think again. Your mother was just the same. Different men in and out of her place all the time. She took my father in that whorehouse of hers, destroyed my family, and you're trying to do the same thing!"

Gina shook her head. "What are you talking about? I don't know anything about what she did. I was forced to go with her till I turned ten, then I tried to stay away from her."

"You're just a little tart. She taught you well, didn't she?"

Their eyes locked.

"Didn't you hear a word I just said? Though I guess it's good to know what your problem is with me. If any of what you said is true."

"My mum told me all about it," Tracy said. "She came home from work early one day and saw my dad come out of your mother's house. My dad acted suspicious when she asked him why he was there, so she followed him one day and waited. I had just turned thirteen at the time. I was devastated when they broke up. If you think you're going to do the same thing to my marriage, think again." Gina had to hold her breath to stop herself chuckling when she saw Tracy's neck wobble. "I'm not letting a disgusting tramp like you near my husband."

Gina clenched her fists and ground her teeth. Her head was pounding harder. She drew closer to Tracy, looked her square in the eye. Neither of them moved or blinked.

"I don't care what you and the people in this village think of me." Gina's voice was low. "I'm not going to stop what I'm doing, and the lot of you can make up any assumptions that come to mind. What happened between your father and Karen had nothing to do with me. I didn't know anything about it till you just mentioned it."

Tracy tutted and rolled her eyes.

"I've done nothing wrong. Now get out of my house!"

Behind her, Gina heard Toby scratch the door, wanting to come in.

"You were seen talking to Colin, smiling at him all the time, flirting," Tracy said. "You think you're so glamorous, don't you? With your blonde hair, walking around with next to nothing on."

Toby was frantically scratching at the back door.

"I'm not after your husband!" Gina looked Tracy up and down, her heart hammering. "If I was, I'd have had him by now."

Tracy looked ready to explode.

Toby was now barking.

"You can let yourself out!" Gina said, and turned away.

As she approached the kitchen, something slammed into her back. Her head hit the door. Everything went hazy for a few seconds. As she turned around, she felt a second blow, this time on the side of her head. Gina fell sideways against the door, her head throbbing. She shook her head to clear it and rounded on Tracy, pushing her as hard as she could. But Tracy didn't move very far, and swung at Gina. Gina moved her head aside and felt the breeze of Tracy's fist as it missed her jaw by inches. She swung a fist of her own and caught Tracy just below her eye, then kicked the back of her leg. Tracy buckled. Sensing she had the upper hand, Gina pushed her towards the front door—but Tracy elbowed her in the mouth. Blood ran down her lip. Tracy forced her against the wall and wrapped her hands around her throat. Gina started choking as Tracy squeezed hard, but managed to knee her in the stomach, causing Tracy to wince in pain. Gina punched her in the jaw—now Tracy's mouth was bleeding too—then grabbed the woman's fingers and bent them back hard. Tracy screamed.

Gina led Tracy to the front door, not letting go of her fingers until she was outside, then slammed the door shut, leant against it and wiped her mouth with her hand.

"You think this is the end of it?" Tracy yelled through the door. "I'll get you for this, bitch! Just you wait—I'm going to really fuck you over! You're done!" Tracy banged on the door, then Gina heard her storm off and slam her own door.

Gina stood against the door with her hand on her chest. Her heart was racing. Her lip was cut open and sore. Her head throbbed violently. She went to the kitchen and let in Toby, who had been barking and crying for ten minutes, then cleaned herself up and gave him some food.

She poured a glass of red wine and drank it in one swoop, still seething at what had happened—the fight she'd had with Tracy and the things she'd been accused of.

Gina threw the glass at the wall. It shattered into little pieces.

She went to the living room, buried her head in a cushion and screamed as hard as she could. Tears streamed down her face. Toby came in, jumped up on her lap, and Gina cuddled him tight as he nestled into her arms.

CHAPTER SEVEN

When Gina woke up on Sunday morning, her jaw was sore and bruised. She looked a mess. But she did her morning routine, took Toby for his walk, then set up her massage table.

Sue showed up on time and hugged her, making her feel better, but she pulled her head away when Sue touched her bruise.

"I heard about what happened with Tracy," Sue said. "It was the talk of coffee morning after the service. We can cancel if you don't feel up to it."

"No, that's alright. I'll be fine once the meds start working," Gina said, then told her side of the story to Sue. "You were there, you heard me."

"Well, under normal circumstances, maybe it wasn't such a good idea, knowing what Tracy is like, but with the drinks flowing…"

"I would've offered him a massage if I'd been completely sober."

Sue raised her eyebrows. "Wow, you are brave."

"I bet Tracy made me look a right bitch?"

"Well. Yes, she did. She can be convincing, let me tell you."

"I don't want to know what she told everyone. They can think what they like."

Gina wanted to ask Sue about what Tracy had told her regarding Karen, but that could wait until she'd done the massage.

Sue lay face down on the table then unclipped her bra. Gina lit her candles, dimmed the lights, and put on soft instrumental music to set the mood.

The session lasted thirty minutes, after which Sue slowly got up. "Thanks, Gina. That's a lot better. I can't tell you how much more relaxed I feel."

While Sue got dressed, Gina went to make two coffees. She had about an hour before her first client arrived, so she took the opportunity to ask Sue if she knew what Karen had done to have affected Tracy so much.

Sue looked at her awkwardly. "Yes, I did hear about it. I didn't say anything because I didn't want to upset you. It's personal, you know."

With a wry smile, Gina put her hand on Sue's arm. "It's okay. I didn't like Karen. She tortured me—not physically, though I got more than my fair share of smacks from her."

"Well… I heard she had different partners."

"Yes, I know," Gina said. "I know she had a few affairs in her time. Believe me, I was the result of one of them." She laughed nervously.

"She had an affair with Tracy's father," Sue said. "When Tracy was about thirteen years old."

Gina felt a shockwave rip through her.

"Are you alright?" Sue said.

"Yes. I thought Tracy was making it up."

"No, I don't think she was."

"I don't know why I'm surprised. Nothing that Karen did should surprise me. Tracy shouldn't take her anger out on me, though. She called me a tramp!"

"She thinks you're after her husband," Sue said.

"But I'm not! It was an innocent offer. If it came out as flirtatious, it wasn't meant to be. It must have been the drink."

"I know that," Sue said. "But she obviously thinks otherwise."

"I'm amazed Colin told her about it, knowing what she's like."

"I don't think he did tell her. I don't think he'd want the aggravation."

Gina frowned. "Then how did she know, Sue?"

"I'm pretty sure it was one of those women sitting near us—you know, the ones with the child. They're quite friendly with Tracy. Maybe you should keep a low profile, try to stay out of her way."

"Maybe I should carry on as normal, Sue! I've done nothing wrong, so I'm not steering clear of anybody. I'm not afraid of her."

Sue got up, and Gina followed her to the door. "Are you still coming to see Dr Southwell with me tomorrow?"

"Yes, of course I am," Sue said, then added, "You want to put some makeup on that bruise."

Gina touched the bruise on her face. She had ten minutes before her first client arrived—enough time to go to her bedroom and apply concealer.

***

When the doorbell rang, Gina took one more look in the mirror to make sure she was presentable, and was relieved to find that she couldn't see the bruise. She went downstairs and opened the door to her first client of the day: a slim man with short grey hair, wearing a green T-shirt and navy shorts. He was a solicitor who worked over twelve hours a day during the week, and he'd been coming to Gina every Sunday afternoon for the last few weeks. After him came a schoolteacher, a woman the same age as Gina. Both were satisfied with the service, which pleased her. Once her work was done, she snuggled up to her beloved Toby and forgot the poison of the world.

CHAPTER EIGHT

Gina kissed Toby goodbye and walked out, admiring the work she'd done on her front garden the previous day, mowing her lawn and attending to her flowers and plants.

"You worked hard yesterday," Sue said. "Looks splendid. I thought you would've stayed indoors, with what happened on Saturday."

"I felt like doing the garden after I'd finished with my clients. I didn't have anything else planned, and I'm not hiding from her or the other neighbours."

As they walked towards the bus stop, Gina noticed Sue looked sombre. "Everything alright, Sue?"

"Well… It's the anniversary today."

Gina put her hand to her mouth. "Oh God, I'm sorry. Your husband had his terrible accident." She embraced Sue. "I can't believe it's been three years already."

Then she remembered that Sue's father had passed away six months later. "How's your mum doing?"

"She's not doing too good. I'll probably have to go live with her before long. Either that or move her into a care home."

Gina's heart broke for Sue; her life had been so full of tragedy. She'd also confessed to Gina, once, that she'd had a miscarriage and was then unable to have children.

"We don't want to miss the bus," Sue said. "You'll be late for your appointment."

"If you need to be with your mum, I can manage."

"No, I spoke to her this morning—she's fine. I'll go and see her later. I want to come with you."

One bus ride later and they were at the clinic. Gina checked in and sat down. She bit her tongue, trying so hard not to scream at the little boy happily playing with some toy bricks while giving his vocal cords plenty of exercise. After what seemed like forever, and with the child's voice stuck in her head, Gina was called in.

Dr Southwell—tall and tanned, with short black hair—greeted them with his broad smile. Gina introduced Sue and they both sat. Silence filled the room. Gina stared at the floor. She waited for Dr Southwell to start, but no one spoke.

"One of our neighbours died," she said eventually.

"Sorry to hear that," Dr Southwell said. "Had they been ill?"

"No. She… had an accident, or maybe she took her own life. I… I don't know."

"Was she a good friend of yours?"

"No," Gina said. "We didn't get along that well, actually. We had an argument a few weeks back. I tried to make amends by offering her a massage to help the pain in her legs."

Sue frowned. "I heard you said it was her back."

"I get confused. I thought it was her legs; I can't remember." Gina looked away. "After a while, she agreed, but later that evening she was discovered unconscious on her lawn. She fell out of her top window and died from her injuries."

"Must have been a shock."

Gina looked at Sue. "They think I was responsible."

"Who does?" Southwell said.

"Everyone in the village."

"They don't think that," Sue said.

"They were all watching me that night, whispering. I got taken down the police station for questioning.

Just because someone saw me come out of her house that afternoon."

"You came out of her house," Southwell said. "Doesn't mean anything. Was there any other evidence against you?"

"No. They didn't find anything."

"What was the earlier altercation about?"

"It was over my dog going on the edge of her driveway. Something so stupid."

Gina told Dr Southwell about her ordeal at the police station.

"I'm not surprised you had a panic attack in that situation," he said. "You seem alright now."

"It's much lighter in here," Gina said. "There's a big window. Though it's frosted, it lets in light, which makes all the difference."

"The lady was alright when you left after the massage?"

"Yes," Gina said. "She was fine, said what I did helped a bit."

"Then your conscience is clear. You've done nothing wrong. The number of people I meet who say they want to end their life… However, usually the people who go through with it don't say anything. They're the ones to watch."

"I learned that as well."

"Anything else happen?" Southwell said.

"No, nothing," Gina said. Sue looked at her pointedly.

They both left the clinic and walked towards the main part of town.

"Why didn't you mention the fight with Tracy?" Sue said.

"I didn't think there was any need to."

Gina was about to walk on, but Sue pulled her back. "I thought you always told him everything?"

Gina sighed. "If I tell him I got into a fight, he might think I need respite or something. I'm just afraid I'll be put in that place again. I know he probably wouldn't, but I don't want to take the risk."

"I'm sure he wouldn't, but okay." Sue gave Gina a warm smile. "Are you alright to look in some shops?"

"Sure. I don't want to be too long, though."

Gina spotted a smiley-face badge in a charity shop and bought it for Sue. She was glad to see a smile across Sue's face when she pinned the badge on her shirt.

"You're the best friend I've ever had," Gina said.

Sue gave Gina a big hug. "Same here."

"I just hope it stays that way."

"What do you mean?" Sue said. "I'm not going anywhere. Are you?"

"No, course not. It's just…"

"Just what? Come on—tell me, Gina."

"You know what I'm like. So much goes through my mind. She might try to drive a wedge between us. You said yourself she's very persuasive."

"Tracy will not drive me against you, Gina. She can be persuasive and controlling, yes, but not with me."

"You mean she hasn't tried already?"

"No. I've no doubt she will try at some point, but I tell you, Gina, she won't succeed. That's a damn promise."

They were soon done in town, and Gina was relieved to be off the bus and back in the village. However, when they reached her house, she stopped at the gate just as she heard Sue gasp.

Gina's stomach churned; her blood boiled.

She slowly walked up her garden, brushing the dirt off her path with her feet and treading on the stems of her squashed flowers. Tears streamed down her face as she felt Sue's hand on her shoulder. Her eyes were locked on her front door: the once smart sky-blue colour now had the word SLUT across it in red spray paint.

"Who did this?" Sue said.

"We know who's responsible, don't we?" Gina's voice quivered.

She went inside. Toby jumped up at her, but she didn't greet him with her usual enthusiasm.

"I'll make a drink," Sue said.

Gina sat down in her chair, shaking. Toby nestled his head against her. She stroked him without even realising what she was doing.

She took the coffee from Sue and held the mug tight by the handle.

"You should report it," Sue said.

"What's the point?" Gina sipped her coffee, wishing it was something stronger. "How can they prove it was her?"

"I don't think Tracy would do something like that," Sue said. "That's the work of kids or teenagers, not something a fifty-plus-year-old woman would do."

"Kids?" Gina chuckled. "Why me? Why my garden and not yours, or hers or anyone else's?"

Sue looked away. "I still think you should report it. Just see what they say."

"I found what I thought would be a quiet little village. Live a quiet life, run a small business from home. I love this house; it's the perfect size for me. And yet I'm getting more crap thrown at me than ever. Best go and clean it up." She stormed into the kitchen to fetch a broom, dustpan and brush.

"You don't want to clean it up until the police have seen it," Sue said. "Report it, Gina!"

"Alright, I will."

She jumped a little as Sue's phone rang. While Sue took the call, Gina went to the living room and called the police.

After she had reported it, Gina returned to the kitchen and almost bumped into Sue.

"Sorry, I need to go," Sue said. "My mum needs me. Just wait for the police, and don't be so quick to blame Tracy. It was just kids, I'm sure."

Gina followed her out and saw Detective Carter had arrived.

"I didn't expect to see you, Detective," she said. "I thought they'd send a normal policeman."

"I'm not normal?" Carter said.

Gina tutted. "You know what I mean."

"Uniformed police," Carter said. "I heard on the radio you made a complaint; I wasn't far away, so I told them I'd attend."

"Look at what she did to my door."

"Let's not jump to conclusions, Miss Wilkinson. This is probably just the work of kids pulling a prank."

Gina folded her arms, her eyes locked on his. "I don't see anyone else's garden being vandalised with disgusting words sprayed on their door."

"We get a lot of graffiti—though not necessarily on people's doors, I'll admit. I'll take some pictures and look into it."

While Carter got his phone out, Gina went and got some cloths and cleaning spray. Once he'd finished photographing the door, she scrubbed as hard as she could, but the spray paint wouldn't come off.

Gina was getting frustrated.

"It doesn't look like it will come off," Carter said. "You might have to paint the door."

Gina stopped scrubbing and took some deep breaths to calm herself.

"What a mess."

Gina's head jerked up to see who'd spoken.

Tracy stood looming. She tutted. "Kids," she said.

Gina balled her fists.

"You need to clean that up—you're ruining the good name of the village."

Gina bit her tongue hard.

"Just look at my neatly mowed lawn and my beautiful flowers, my two little gnomes in front of the window."

Gina started shaking as she followed Tracy's gaze to her door.

"Somebody obviously knows you." Tracy lowered her voice to a whisper. "That's what happens when you follow in the footsteps of your mother. You can say what you like, but we know what really goes on, don't we? How many families are you attempting to destroy?"

Gina stormed inside and went for her medicine cupboard in the kitchen. She swallowed three Valium and leant against the sink.

That word got stuck in her mind. *Slut!* She pounded the sink. *They all think I'm a slut!* Her eyes welled up.

"I'll be off now, Miss Wilkinson."

Gina jumped and spun around. Carter was standing behind her.

"Hey… I'll do what I can," he said. "I spoke to Mrs Harper, but she doesn't know anything."

"How surprising," Gina said.

CHAPTER NINE

"Not going to Annie's funeral, Gina?" Sue said.

"Erm… No, I can't. Sorry… I just can't. I want to get this door painted, anyway."

"You wouldn't pay your respects to someone you murdered, would you?"

Gina ignored Tracy's remark behind her and carried on painting.

"I don't know why you're painting your door; it described you perfectly."

She spun around, but Tracy was already walking towards the church with Sue close behind. A group of people lingered outside. Gina wondered if she was the only one who wasn't attending.

She went to carry on but was distracted when a hearse parked across the street, along with another car. Gina stood and watched two men and two women come out of Annie's and line up behind the hearse. A man in a grey overcoat and top hat walked in front of it all the way to the village church. Gina watched until everyone had filtered inside.

***

Over the next two weeks, Gina didn't leave the house apart from taking Toby for walks and going to the village store. She had a few clients at the weekend, but spent most of her time reading and doing her colouring books. Her garden was tidy again, minus the flowers that had been destroyed. She was on her guard the whole time, expecting something nasty to happen to her. Tracy's threat was replaying in her mind; she had trouble coming her way. *You're done!* What did she mean by that?

Gina was still convinced Tracy was responsible for the wreck in her garden. Even if it had been kids, she was certain Tracy must have been involved. Maybe she'd offered them money or something.

However, nothing else had happened. She hadn't seen Tracy since the day of Annie's funeral.

Gina looked in her diary and saw she had a new client booked that afternoon. She couldn't remember booking anyone, which made her feel uneasy, but the name and time were there.

She had everything set when the doorbell rang. A man who looked to be in his early twenties, with short ginger hair and heavy stubble, stood at the door.

"Jim Atkins. I have an appointment."

Gina smelled the alcohol straight away. There was a bad vibe about him.

Nevertheless, she led him into the living room and told him to take his shirt off, if he wanted to, and lie face down. "I'll be right back."

She went to the kitchen, her nerves on edge; she had a bad feeling about this man. She took an extra antidepressant, then went back to the living room.

The man was just standing there, looking around the room.

"Are you alright?" she asked.

"Yeah, fine."

"You want to lie down, Mr Atkins?"

"Call me Jim," he told her. Again the smell of alcohol on his breath, but he seemed in control of himself. "I… heard…" He hesitated. "You give other services to your male clients?"

"Really?" Her voice went high. "Who told you that?" There was a sudden knot in her stomach.

"Just… Someone I know told me you offer a bit of fun after the massage." Atkins moved closer; Gina backed away. "Why don't we forget the massage and get comfy on your sofa, or we can go upstairs? I don't mind. I don't need to catch my train for a few hours, so I have plenty of time."

She sighed. "I'm sorry, Mr Atkins, but there's been a misunderstanding here. I *don't* do that! Whoever told you I did is mistaken." *I wonder who that was*, she thought. "I'm sure you can find places for that sort of thing, Mr Atkins. If not, try the streets."

He backed her up against the door.

Gina took deep breaths to stem the panic that rose up inside her. She turned her face away as she felt his breath, then shoved him hard, opened the door and went for the kitchen—but he grabbed her hair, pulled her back, slammed the door and pushed her against it.

"But I'm ready for you." He grabbed her hand and put it against his crotch. "Feel," he told her, pressing her hand harder against him.

She tried to pull away, but he was strong.

"*No!*" she yelled, and yanked her hand away hard.

He put his hand on her breast. Gina pushed him as hard as she could, but he came at her again, holding her shoulders, trying to kiss her. Another whiff of his breath made her stomach heave. She turned her face and he licked her cheek. Gina gagged as he continued to kiss her. She tried with all her might to push him away, but Atkins held her tighter. He drew close to her again, but she put her hand on his face and pinched his cheek. He knocked her arm out of the way and rammed her head against the wall, making her light-headed for a few seconds. As her vision righted itself, he pulled the back of her hair and slapped her cheek. The more she tried to fight him, the more aggressive he became. Gina screamed, but it was muffled by the tight grip of his hand over her mouth.

"You don't come on to me then reject me like this." Atkins's hand went to his back pocket.

"I never came on to you." She barely got her words out.

Her eyes widened. A shiny blade glinted brightly inches from her face.

"You're a little fighter, aren't you?" Spit flew on her face as he spoke, and Gina thought she was going to be sick—which wouldn't have been so bad, as he was still pressed up against her.

"You're going to give me what I want!"

She moved her hand onto his to stop it sliding down the front of her shorts. It was a natural reaction, like slamming on the brake of a car to prevent an accident. She pulled back as she felt the sharp blade against her throat.

Gina closed her eyes as his hand went inside her shorts, then her knickers.

"Wait!" she squealed. "Massage first—then we'll have fun." She faked a smile.

She wasn't sure if he'd take notice of what she said—but he stopped, took his hand away and backed off slightly. She had to calm him down, take control of the situation. He was riled up, and she wouldn't get rid of him till he got what he wanted. The front door was unlocked. Her mind was running overtime. *It would take only a few seconds to run next door to Sue's and bang on her door for help.*

"Massage first," she said.

Atkins eyed her suspiciously but backed off a little more. "Then we can have fun?"

Gina felt Toby brush past her leg. "Oh yes," she said. "We have to be calm and relaxed—more enjoyable that way. Just lie face down on the table."

He backed away a couple of steps, closed his knife and put it in his pocket.

"I'll be a few minutes," she said. "I need to take some tablets to calm myself down."

She went back out to the hallway. There was enough distance between them for her to get to Sue's.

She had opened the front door when she heard his voice behind her.

"Hello, boy. What a lovely dog you have—so small, light and fluffy."

The words hit her like a bolt of lightning. Gina froze.

She turned and saw Atkins with Toby in his arms, stroking him gently.

"Please put him down." She was shaking, tears rolling down her cheeks.

"Shut the door and lock it!" he snapped. "It would be so unfortunate if something happened to such a small cute dog. I mean… His bones, for example, will break very easily."

"I'll call the police," Gina said.

"It was a complete accident," Atkins said. "I accidentally trod on his leg while he was on the floor asleep. It's your word against mine. Lock the fucking door, now!"

Gina bolted the door and put the chain across, then followed him to the kitchen.

"Lock the back door as well."

"It's too hot to have all the doors closed."

Gina went to take Toby off him, but he backed away and grabbed Toby's paw. "Lock it!"

She locked the door, then went to take Toby.

Again, he backed off.

"Please give him to me."

"You get yourself ready, and I'll take care of the little fellow. No tricks—it would be a shame to break him."

Gina cringed as he kissed Toby's head and went into the living room. She leant against the kitchen table. Hot blood boiled inside her. With Atkins out of sight, she looked for her phone, but realised it was in the living room. She gulped down some Valium and splashed cold water on her face, but she wanted to shower, to scrub herself clean. The thought of having to put her hands on that man made her sick to her stomach. She knew she had to, though. He was in there with Toby.

Still shaking, she breathed deeply and started to calm down. She grabbed her oil and went into the living room.

Atkins was lying on his stomach. The candles were lit and the soft music was playing in the background. There were two spots on his back, and her stomach churned again at the thought of touching him. Watching Toby lying on the floor, she thought about making her escape while Atkins was on the massage table, but she would have to unlock the door—which would give Atkins enough time to get hold of him. Even if she picked up Toby first, it was too risky. Toby was everything, her precious little baby.

Gina closed her eyes as she started slowly rubbing Atkins's back and shoulders. She added the oil and was pleased to find that as time went on, he became more relaxed. She started talking to him dreamily in a quiet, soft voice while rubbing him gently, stepping out of herself as if she'd gone into another dimension. All the panic she'd felt came out of her, and she felt much more relaxed.

"Where are you going on the train?" she said.

"To see my parents in Ramsgate." Atkins's voice was calm, so different to his sharp, aggressive tone earlier.

Gina added more oil and continued to rub his back and shoulders, then suddenly bent down and whispered in his ear.

When she'd finished, she rubbed the excess oil off his back. It was then Gina came back to her normal self; she spotted her phone on the mantelpiece, and Toby sitting on her chair. Her heart started racing. She grabbed her phone and texted Sue to come over ASAP, then hurried into the kitchen to wash her hands. After picking up Toby from her chair and putting him in the garden, she checked her phone. It had been over ten minutes since she'd texted Sue, but as yet there was no response.

In the living room, Atkins was getting to his feet. She unlocked the front door and watched him stretch.

Her heart rate was accelerating; Sue should have been here by now. Gina was screaming in her head. *Come on, Sue! Hurry up!*

Toby came back and stood by her, so she picked him up.

"I feel great," Atkins said. He sounded calmer, and she felt some relief.

"Your shirt's over there." She pointed to the sofa.

He grabbed it and shrugged it onto his shoulders. For a moment, she thought he would put it on and be done, but dread gripped her as he turned towards her, his buttons still open and a lecherous grin on his face.

Gina started to feel dizzy. The thought of his hands on her made her insides turn to jelly. Her back was against the wall, and he was inches from her. She glanced at the door; still no sign of Sue. His hand came towards her, and she gasped… but he just stroked Toby's head gently.

Gina went to open the door for him to leave, but he got there first. Panic hit her in the chest; was he going to lock it?

But he opened the door and left.

CHAPTER TEN

"I need a drink," Gina said.

"I'll have some tea if you're making some."

She looked back at Sue. "I need something stronger."

Gina poured some whisky and gulped it down. She stood there shaking, banging her head with her fists.

Sue grabbed her face, and their eyes locked on each other. "What on earth's wrong with you?"

Gina told her everything.

Sue reached for her phone, but Gina grabbed her arm.

Sue looked at her askance. "You have to report it."

"He didn't rape me."

Gina poured two more glasses of whisky. She handed one to Sue, then went to the living room and gulped down the other one.

"You still need to report it," Sue said. "You can't let him get away with that."

Gina put away her massage table, then went into the bathroom to splash cold water on her face; she could hear Sue talking to someone the living room. She hurried back just as Sue hung up her phone.

"What are you doing?"

"I've called the police."

"What the hell for?"

"It's the right thing to do. He assaulted you. Can't let him get away with something like that. What if he does it to someone else?"

"I guess you're right," Gina said. "It does need to be reported. I can still feel his hands on me. I feel dirty."

"Could've been worse if not for your quick thinking," Sue said. She pointed at Gina's leg. "Did he do that?"

Gina looked down and saw a large bruise on her thigh. "It wasn't there before, so he must have. He had his hands all over me. I was so preoccupied in fighting him off, and he moved so quickly."

***

Gina showed the two uniformed police officers into the living room. She went through her ordeal again, explaining what had happened in detail. However, she declined the offer to go to the hospital, so the female officer examined her bruise and took a photo.

When everyone had left, she went straight for the shower. She washed her face several times where his tongue had been, and scrubbed her legs and all the places in between where his hands had touched. Her head was pounding, and she winced when she felt the bruise on her leg.

Gina settled in front of the TV, watching *The FBI Files* and *Crime Scene Investigation*. Flashes of Atkins touching her filled her mind. She had palpitations, and her eyes burned with tears. She turned the volume up a little. Her eyelids drooped as the sleeping pills she'd taken worked their way through, and her hand rose and fell with Toby's breathing…

Suddenly, Gina opened her eyes. She was still in her chair; the sun was shining through her curtains, the TV was still on, and Toby was barking at the front door. Fumbling for her phone, she tried to focus her eyes: 9.45 a.m. The doorbell rang, followed by banging that hammered through her head. She staggered towards the door, squinting in the bright light.

Carter and Kene were standing before her. She let them in, put Toby in the back garden, then returned to the kitchen, where Kene was having a good look around. Her Valium was on the table. The memory of the interrogation flooded her mind.

"You take many of these?" Kene was studying the box.

"I take a few a day." *Plus a few more.*

"Miss Wilkinson, we're here about the complaint you made last night."

She eyed Carter, but he looked away.

"Mr Atkins was picked up yesterday evening. He was just leaving to see his parents." Gina barely understood Kene's deep Scottish accent. "He said it was a misunderstanding. Told us you came on to him. He didn't force you to do anything."

"He's lying. He pinned me against the wall. I tried to fight him, but he was strong. The bruise on my leg was down to him."

"He said it got a bit rough, but you enjoyed it," Kene said. He turned to Carter, who was leafing through his notebook. "That's right, isn't it, Detective?"

"Er, yes," Carter said. "Bit rough, but you told him he could have the massage first, then you could both have fun."

Gina folded her arms.

Carter continued reading his notes. "He said the massage was fantastic, but then your neighbour turned up, so he left."

Gina's face was in her hands; her chest got tight and she bit her lip. "He had me against the wall. His hands were all over me, squeezing my breasts and shoved down my shorts." Her face grew hot as her voice got louder. "I said I'd give him the massage first and have fun afterwards to make him stop. He was really wound up; I had to calm him somehow. I sent Sue a text. You can ask her."

"We did, before we came here," Carter said. "She told us you were in a state and you were angry."

"Of course I was angry!" Gina shouted. "I've had a lot of male clients, but none of them have ever laid a finger on me."

"We spoke to other neighbours as well," Kene said. "We had a chat with Tracy Harper."

Gina closed her eyes, dreading what was going to come next.

"Mrs Harper knows James Atkins. She and her husband see him at the pub quite a bit. She said he's a charming, very polite man. When he's had a few drinks he's a bit loud, but not aggressive."

Gina faced Kene. "He sexually assaulted me with intent to rape! I did what I could to stop him!"

Kene sighed. "I'm sorry, Miss Wilkinson, but it's your word against his. Plus, there's little evidence, given your refusal to attend hospital yesterday. I'm afraid we don't have the resources to pursue this case, as there would be very little chance of a conviction."

Gina heard him without taking in what he said.

"Maybe you should get into another kind of business, Miss Wilkinson. You might not get into this kind of situation."

She stared at his face. His double chin, full of sticky grey stubble.

"Get the hell out of my house!"

CHAPTER ELEVEN

The door slammed. Gina leant against it.

Then she heard Tracy's voice outside. "Someone's not happy."

Gina put her ear against the door.

"We can't do anything about her complaint, Mrs Harper. No real evidence."

"She brings it on herself, Detective. She has all sorts going in and out of her place."

Gina's instincts told her to walk away, but she couldn't help herself.

"She's in a dangerous business. I told her she should do something else, or work in a proper spa facility with other people," Tracy said. "I heard months ago she works from home because of her mental health issues—one of the neighbours told me. But I think she plays on it for sympathy. There's nothing wrong with her."

Gina's knuckles were white as she stared into her own eyes in the hallway mirror.

Her phone rumbled in her pocket. No name, just a number.

"Hello?"

"It's James Atkins."

She froze and said nothing, grinding her teeth as he breathed deep in her ear. She could still feel his disgusting tongue on her face.

"Are you there?"

"Yes. What do you want?" she said, a mix of panic and anger in her voice.

"You sound different," he said. "Anyway, I just wanted to apologise for the misunderstanding we had yesterday. I'd had quite a bit to drink, and I thought you'd be up for some fun. I was shocked when I got dragged down the police station."

"You assaulted me!"

"I was meant to go to my parents' last night, but I was chucked in a police cell instead," Atkins said, totally ignoring Gina's last comment.

Gina took a very deep breath, then brought her voice to a calm whisper. Unblinking, she whispered something to Atkins, then hung up.

***

Later that afternoon, Gina was preparing a chicken with salad for dinner when her phone went off. She jumped but was relieved to see Sue's name pop up.

"Have you seen the news?" Sue asked.

"Er, no. What's happened?"

She put on the TV and selected the local news channel. Across the bottom of the screen, scrolling yellow text read:

INCIDENT AT CANTERBURY STATION

"It looks like that creep you had at your place yesterday," Sue said. "The one that assaulted you."

A photo came up on the screen. Gina put her hand to her mouth as she listened to the report.

"There was disruption to services at Canterbury station earlier today as a man is believed to have jumped from the platform into the path of a moving train, and was sadly killed. Police have released these CCTV images of the man, thought to be in his twenties, and are appealing for witnesses to the incident. In particular, they would like to speak to an individual he is thought to have called from his mobile phone shortly before his death."

Gina turned the TV off.

"Why would he do that?" Sue said. "I wonder who he called? His parents?"

"I don't know," Gina said.

Gina had a very disturbed night; she tossed and turned so much that Toby ended up sleeping on the floor. She had visions of Atkins lying mangled on the tracks, a voice in her head saying how much he deserved it after what he put her through. Her own dreamy voice echoed through her, saying she'd wished for this to happen, that she *told* him to jump in front of that train. The voice kept repeating: *you told him, you told him.*

"NO!" she screamed, and sat up.

She was breathless, like she'd been on a long run. She checked her phone; it was just before six. Her nightgown was sticking to her, so she headed for the shower.

***

Later that afternoon, Gina was walking home from the village shop with Toby when she spotted Chief Inspector Kene and DS Carter talking to Tracy in the street. Her heart sank.

As she approached her garden, Tracy charged at her. "What did you say to him?" she screamed. The detectives grabbed her, holding her back.

Gina shook her head and opened her door.

"We'd like a word, Miss Wilkinson," Kene said.

Gina rolled her eyes, and the detectives followed her to the kitchen. "Why don't you move in?" she said. "You keep finding your way here."

Kene ignored her comment, but Carter's hearty chuckle earned him a sharp look. "We need to ask you a few questions involving the late Mr Atkins. You know what happened?"

She sighed. "Yes. I saw it on the news."

"Apparently you were the last person to have contact with the deceased."

Gina shrugged. "What if I was? So what?"

Carter was about to speak, but Kene put his hand up. "There's a few things that don't add up."

"Such as?"

"You claimed he attacked you, but you still gave him the massage he came for. And it appears that just before he leapt in front of the train, the number he called was yours."

"How do you know he called me?"

"His mobile was damaged beyond repair, but we went to his phone company and they told us. We needed to know the last person he had contact with."

"So was I somehow responsible for pushing him in front of the train?" Gina tapped her fingers on the tabletop.

"We know you weren't there," Kene said. "I just want to know what was said on the phone. How did he sound? Remorseful, depressed?"

"I can't remember."

"Sudden memory loss, eh? You led him on, then changed your mind, for whatever reason." Kene's face got redder. "When he called you, probably to apologise, you perhaps told him how shameful and disgusting he was? Perhaps you suggested that he deserved to be punished? Perhaps even to die? You certainly appear to have no compassion for him, no remorse, and no regard for human life."

"Do you know how that sounds?" Gina folded her arms and drew closer to Kene. "I didn't lead him on. He was a disgusting man who hurt and touched me. So if you're asking if I have any remorse for him, personally? I don't! I can't remember what conversation we had on the phone. But even if I told him I wished he was dead, why would he take his own life?"

"How convenient. You remember all he did to you but can't remember any conversations. I just find it strange that two people you recently had contact with are now dead."

"You have no proof I did anything to anyone."

"Miss Wilkinson, what did Mr Atkins say on the phone? I don't believe you can't remember; it was just yesterday."

"I'm trying to remember, but I just can't."

"Do you only take prescribed drugs?"

"Yes. You think I'm on cocaine or heroin, then?"

"Your mother was Karen Barker? She was well known to us years ago. I was in uniform at that time."

She glanced at Carter. "Small world."

"Well. I'm sure we'll be meeting again, Miss Wilkinson. Be sure to let us know any information if your memory does come back."

Gina wasn't lying. She remembered some of the call—Atkins apologising for what he said was a misunderstanding, and saying he wanted to make it up to her—but the rest was a blur. She couldn't remember what she'd said to him. Would she tell him to jump in front of a train? Possibly—she loathed him for putting his hands on her. But why would he actually do it? She shook her head. She wasn't responsible for what happened.

CHAPTER TWELVE

Dr Southwell's receptionist stared at Toby, then at Gina.

"He's an assistance dog," Gina said, before the woman could say anything.

"Take a seat, please."

Gina sat down, putting Toby on her lap and stroking him gently. When a man came out of Dr Southwell's office, the receptionist went in and closed the door; Gina knew she'd gone to tell the doctor about Toby. She came out a minute later. "You can go in now."

Gina went in, and Southwell greeted her in his usual smiling manner, then bent down to stroke Toby. "Ah, isn't he a gorgeous little fellow."

"He is, yes. He's my absolute world."

"Where is your friend today?"

"Oh, Sue couldn't make it, which is why I brought Toby. He's an assistance dog, so he can go everywhere with me."

Southwell smiled and gently stroked the top of Toby's head. "If having him with you helps, then that can only be a good thing."

"He helps me so much. Many people don't understand how a dog can help if you suffer with anxiety, but he really does."

"I don't really know much about dogs," Southwell said. "However, after what you just told me, I would strongly suggest you keep him with you and take him everywhere you go."

"I didn't even know about assistance dogs until a few months ago. I saw someone with a dog, and their lead had 'assistance dog' on it, so I made some enquiries and managed to get Toby."

"Why is this the first time you've brought him here?"

"Because I'm usually with Sue. She's not that keen on dogs."

Southwell raised his eyebrows. "If you feel more relaxed when he's with you, then you take him, even if you're with Sue. He's an aid, like a walking stick if you have a bad leg. Sue will get used to it." Gina felt like she wanted to cry; chatting with Southwell was more like talking to a friend than a counsellor.

"What's been going on?" Dr Southwell said.

Gina looked up at him. "I don't know where to start." Her voice was shaky.

"Just take your time and start from the beginning."

He was so relaxed, and his voice was so gentle, that she felt completely comfortable. So she told him about the mess in her garden and the word sprayed on her door, then about her ordeal with Atkins and what had happened the next day. She saw no emotion on Dr Southwell's face.

"He jumped in front of a train," she finished.

"Yes, I saw that on the news. But you weren't there. You didn't do anything."

"I was the last person to have contact with him. He called me, but I can't remember the conversation we had. The police think I told him to jump in front of that train. I don't remember saying that. Part of me is sorry for what happened, but there's another part of me that thinks he deserved it."

Southwell stayed silent, but she had his full attention.

"I can still feel his disgusting hands over me. What gives him the right to touch me like that? To shove his hands down my underwear and touch my... well, you know. Then he threatened Toby—he picked him up and threatened to hurt him to make me do what he wanted, the filthy…" She slammed her fists on the table and jumped out of her chair.

Southwell didn't move.

Silence filled the room for a few moments, then Gina sat back down. Breathing heavily, tears rolling down her face, she watched Southwell write in his notebook.

"I don't remember telling him to jump in front of that train." She chuckled. "He wouldn't do it on my command, anyway."

"See—it's not your fault. You're not responsible for what happened," Southwell said. "The fact you can't remember—that's not uncommon. Temporary amnesia can happen, especially if you're really stressed or angry. The words just come out, beyond our control."

"I don't want to go back to that place. It took six months to get out the last time."

Southwell gave a chuckle. "I wouldn't put you in there. Not unless you were a danger to yourself or other people. How often do you get these gaps in your memory?"

"Not that often, as far as I know. Maybe when I'm angry or anxious. Let me think… Well, for example, just over a year ago, I was talking to Sue about something that upset me, and when I spoke to her the next day, she said the tone of my voice had changed and I said things I wouldn't normally say. I tried to remember, but I just drew a blank. She said it was like talking to a different person."

"That's interesting," Southwell said. "Sue is the lady you brought here before?"

"Yes. She's the only friend I have. She knows about my issues anyway, but I think it just shocked her."

"Did it shock you when she told you?"

"Definitely! Scared me as well, especially when I couldn't remember. Two people have died, and my neighbours and the police think I was involved because I was the last person to have contact. So much for moving to a quiet village—or what I thought was quiet."

"I don't think we need to worry about it at this stage. Like you said, there's no evidence, and you weren't even at the station when the man took his life. You've done nothing wrong."

Gina put her head in her hands. "What about Annie? What if I… did it?" She wiped her eyes.

"You didn't do it," Southwell said. "The police found no evidence. You went over in the afternoon, gave her a massage, then left. That's what you said, isn't it?"

"Yes, but—"

"But nothing. One of the neighbours saw you leave, and they saw Annie shut the door. That's true, right?"

"Yes. But when the police questioned me, they said I might have gone back later that evening. What if… What if I went back, got into a fight, pushed her out the window and have no memory of it?"

"Someone would've seen something. They would've heard a scream, and you said nothing was broken or out of place. You're not the kind to hurt people, Gina. You have a mental health condition, and your mind sometimes plays tricks on you."

"I just want people to leave me alone. Especially the police. That Inspector Kene… The guy's just like that old TV detective, Columbo."

Southwell laughed. "My wife loves that programme… Just try to relax. I can't increase the dose of your tablets, as you're on the maximum already. You told me that you love doing craft and things like that?" Gina nodded. "Just keep doing what relaxes you, and I'll see you in a month's time."

CHAPTER THIRTEEN

After her session, Dr Southwell's words kept repeating in her head, making her feel better. There was no evidence she'd done anything wrong, and she concluded that Kene was just a grumpy old policeman who wanted her to confess to everything so it looked good on him. So what if she was the last person to have contact? Didn't mean anything.

Walking through the town centre, she felt hungry. She scooped Toby up in her arms and poked her head into a couple of small cafes, but there were mums chatting away and their babies making noise. Near the end of town, she came across Billy's Diner. She'd never been there before, but there was only one person inside, so she went in.

The waitress, a young girl with fair hair done up in a bun, came towards her with eyes narrowed, staring at Toby; Gina was gearing up for another battle. However, the waitress obviously saw the big black letters on his lead and led her to a small single table next to the window. The seats were long and high-backed, made of leather in a rich red. When Gina sat down, the back of the chair peeked over her head. She felt like she was in her own little bubble. She put Toby next to her and he laid down with his chin on her lap. There were no loud sounds of coffee machines or the clanking of cups and saucers like you get in a lot of cafes. "Blueberry Hill'" by Fats Domino was playing in the background, but it was low enough that it didn't bother her at all. She ordered a large cheeseburger and a coffee with cream.

Gina flicked through the women's magazine she had in her bag. She'd drunk nearly half of her coffee by the time her burger came out and was so hungry that she sighed when she took the first bite, before taking a tiny bit off the edge and giving it to Toby. Halfway through her burger, she heard two women's voices coming towards her. Suddenly uncomfortable, her heart rate sped up as the waitress put the women on the table directly behind where Gina sat. She couldn't mistake the low and hoarse voice: Tracy Harper and her friend Eileen Levin.

Gina was so grateful for the high-backed chairs.

She should have paid her bill and left—but she waved the waitress over, gave her the empty coffee cup and asked for another one, mouthing the words so she wouldn't be heard. She gently stroked the top of Toby's head, wondering what Tracy and Eileen would talk about. Gina knew listening to other people's conversations wasn't the best idea, as she had a strong feeling her name would pop up, but she couldn't help herself. Her eyes rolled and she shook her head when she heard Tracy order a double cheeseburger, large chips and a large chocolate milkshake. Eileen ordered chicken wings with salad and a pot of tea.

"You don't look happy, Tracy."

"Course I'm not happy, you stupid old woman. Look what that cow next door did to poor James. Colin and I are devastated. He was a drinking pal of ours— well, Colin's mostly, but he was a really nice guy. Then she comes along and accuses him of rape or whatever— after *she* leads him on, I might add—and now he's dead."

Gina turned to glare at the back of the chair behind her.

"He took his own life, Tracy. You sure he wasn't on drugs or anything?"

Gina nodded. *Wouldn't surprise me.*

"No way. He liked his drink, yeah, got somewhat loud when he had too many, but never violent. He was a nice young man, helpful too."

Hearing Tracy's muffled voice, Gina smirked.

"I want her gone from our village," Tracy said. "We had a nice, friendly, respectable community, and she's tarnishing it every day. We all know what goes on in that house."

"She has mental health issues, so I understand, and you're only guessing what goes on, Tracy. You have no proof."

"Well, she seems fine to me. She plays on that crap to get attention, make people feel sorry for her. She knows what she's doing. I'm not going to be fooled by her sick games. I think she was responsible for Jim taking his own life. And Annie."

Gina sipped her coffee, eyebrows raised.

"But how? She was nowhere near the station when Jim took his life. Witnesses saw it."

Gina nodded. A thump on the table behind made her jump.

"You want to know how, Eileen? Drugs! I've been thinking about it. That's the only answer. There's no way Annie would jump out that window. You've known her for years. Unless you've gone senile in your old age. I'm surprised you didn't come up with that yourself—you and George were pharmacists."

"George was the pharmacist; I just served behind the counter, and we served to help people, not finish them off. And how would she get Annie and your friend to take the drug?"

"I heard she makes her clients a drink after she's massaged them. And with Annie and Jim she probably put something in there. That's how she did it, I'm sure."

"You're deluded, Tracy. What kind of drug would make someone jump out of a window, or in front of a train? And where would she get it, anyway?"

"Who knows what's out there?" Tracy said. "I wouldn't be surprised if she had all kinds of drugs in that place of hers. If the police could find a reason to search it, I bet they'd find something. She's just like her mother. We have to get rid of her before she gets to anyone else."

"How are you going to do that? I hate to say it, but I think this is becoming an obsession with you, Tracy. That's why you paid those boys to ruin her garden and spray on her door."

"Keep your voice down, you daft old thing! I'm trying to do our community a favour. I see right through that bitch! I know what she's trying to do."

Gina felt a lump in her throat. She'd suspected Tracy was involved, so she wasn't shocked to learn that she had arranged the incident—but hearing her confess still brought back her anger.

"It sounds to me more like you hold a personal grudge against her," Eileen said. "The fact is, you have no real evidence she's done anything to anyone. She seems friendly enough with Sue."

Gina had such an urge to jump out of her seat and pounce on Tracy like a wild dog. But she managed to contain herself by focusing on Toby and stroking his head, which calmed her down a little.

Then Toby sneezed twice.

"Bless you," came Eileen's voice.

Gina held her breath, staring at Toby, who rolled over and laid his back on her leg.

"Whose side are you on?" Tracy said. "I know Sue has been sucked into her sympathy games, but she doesn't seem to be the only one."

"You mean me? I haven't been sucked in," Eileen said. "I'm just stating the facts."

"She's clever," Tracy said, "which makes her more dangerous. Sue's been blinded by her sob stories—she just doesn't realise it. Someone needs to open her eyes."

Eileen sighed. "Let me guess who that someone is."

"Come on," Tracy said. "Let's pay up and get out of here. Gina's just the same as her mother—a homewrecker. I don't care what crap she comes out with. Well, I'm not giving her the satisfaction, that's for sure. I'll be ready for that bitch any time."

Gina heard shuffling; she glanced around and saw them waiting at the till. She gulped down the rest of her coffee, then watched as the two of them walked out, Tracy still nattering away.

"Everything alright, love?"

Gina looked up at the waitress.

"Can I get you anything else?"

"Glass of water, please." Gina didn't feel like leaving yet; she didn't want to bump into Tracy and Eileen walking through town.

"Would your dog like some water?"

"I'm sure he'd love some, thank you."

Gina thought about Karen. Would any of this have been happening if Karen hadn't been with Tracy's father? She'd thought she'd got rid of her, but it seemed her mother was back to haunt her all over again.

CHAPTER FOURTEEN

1976

Gina sat in the living room with her coat on, clutching a bag with some clothes in. She looked at Lynda, tears in her eyes. "She will bring me back, won't she?"

"Of course she will," Lynda said. "She has done all the other times, hasn't she, although I know it's been very late at night on a few occasions. I'm just hoping she'll come for you. The number of times you've sat here all ready, waiting for her, and she never arrived..."

"I hope she doesn't come. I don't want to go with her. She won't bring me back."

Lynda crouched down in front of her. "She's taking you somewhere nice. You'll have a good time, I'm sure."

Gina glared at her and shook her head.

There was a knock at the door, and she jumped.

Karen took Gina's bag and led her away to a yellow Ford Fiesta; Carol was driving. Carol greeted Gina, who returned a hello with a smile.

"Now, Gina," Karen said, "we're going to a nice place over the weekend, and I want you on your best behaviour. If you're naughty, you know what will happen, don't you?" Gina nodded. "You're eight years old now, so you should know how to behave."

The journey took a couple of hours, but Gina enjoyed the scenery flashing past her window. They arrived at what looked to Gina like a big house. They were led to their room, with only two single beds. She was afraid to ask where she was going to sleep.

But she found out later that evening. They were downstairs in the club area when she saw Karen kissing and hugging a man she'd never seen before. He was tall with thin, grey hair.

Gina looked at Carol. "Who's that man?"

"That's Karen's friend."

The more time Gina spent with Carol, the more she liked her. "Where am I sleeping tonight, Auntie Carol? There's only two beds in our room."

Carol hesitated. "Well, Karen will be in the same room as her friend there. She won't be with us. I'll look after you during the night."

Gina gave a bright smile.

***

The following afternoon, Gina was drinking some orange juice when a loud bang made her jump and spill her drink down her white dress.

"Look what you've done to that nice dress, you stupid girl!" Karen yelled so loud the room went quiet. Her words were slurred.

She grabbed Gina's arm and took her to her room—where she took off her dress, forced her over her knee and smacked her legs seven times, before throwing her on the bed. Gina fell off the other side.

***

Lynda opened the door to find Gina and Carol standing on the doorstep. Gina trudged in, her head down.

"Mrs Wilkinson," Carol said. "Please... Do whatever you can to hold on to this child. She can't live with my sister—not ever."

CHAPTER FIFTEEN

Exhausted, Gina took off Toby's lead as soon as they walked in the front door. She checked her diary and saw Sue was coming over tonight. She'd forgotten about it with everything going on, but laid out snacks and wine before taking her evening medication and settling gratefully into her chair with Toby.

When Sue came to the door, they hugged, being careful not to squash Toby between them. Sue gave him a small pat on the head before Gina put him down; she always got the impression Sue didn't like dogs in general.

Gina poured them a glass of wine each, then told Sue about what had happened at the diner.

"I think Tracy's got issues of her own," Sue said.

"Eileen thought the same thing. I couldn't believe it when I heard what she was saying."

"Let me get this straight," Sue said. "Tracy thinks you put a drug in Annie and that man's drink, causing them to commit suicide?"

Gina nodded. "She thinks I have all kinds of illegal drugs stashed here. The only drugs I have are what the doctor prescribes me. Anyway, I didn't make either of them a drink after their session—Annie didn't want one, and as for that disgusting Atkins guy, I couldn't wait to get him out the door, so why would I offer him a drink?"

"What else did she say?"

"She wants me out of the village," Gina said. "But I figured that already. I'm not going anywhere. I'm not letting her tell me what I should or shouldn't do."

"Are you going to carry on with your work here?"

"Yes. But for now, I'll just have ladies only. After what happened, I'm not comfortable having men in the house."

"Don't blame you for that," Sue said. "Must've been terrifying."

"Yeah, it certainly was." Gina gave a nervous chuckle. "Also, having just women for a while might calm down the rumours about me and what goes on here. Well, I say that—but knowing her next door, she'll probably start new rumours saying I've turned or something." She laughed.

"It's good to see you laughing," Sue said. "It's been a while."

"Dr Southwell said try to relax, do what makes me relaxed and comfortable. I'm not going to concern myself with other people and what they think of me. He said, *you've done nothing wrong!* The tone in his voice was quite abrupt, like he was driving the words into my head."

"I guess you told him about what happened with Atkins and what he did after?"

"Yeah. We talked about that for some time. He saw it in the paper. He understood the ordeal I'd been through. He told me to keep taking the anxiety tablets and prescribed me more Valium." Gina sighed. "I also told him about the gaps in my memory." She glanced anxiously at Sue.

Sue leant forward. "What gaps?"

"I have gaps in my memory," Gina said. "I told you about it, remember?"

They stared at each other.

"Sometimes I say or do something and have no memory of it," she continued.

"Oh, yes," Sue said. "I remember now – after you had that funny turn."

"Yes, the funny turn. I hope I'm not passing whatever I've got on to you." Sue looked puzzled. "Gaps in your memory, I mean."

They both laughed.

"What did the doctor say?" Sue said.

"Not much. He asked how often I get these gaps. I told him not often, which is true. Mainly when I'm really stressed out."

"I had no idea," Sue said. "He didn't seem too concerned, I take it?"

Gina shook her head. "No. He said it was probably nothing to worry about. I feel so comfortable talking to him," she said. "He really listens to me."

"I thought Dr Southwell was very nice," Sue said. "Bit of a dish, actually."

Gina grinned. "You really like the guy, don't you?"

Sue turned her head away. "Not like that."

"I can tell." Gina's grin widened.

"Don't you like him?"

"I've been down that road—never again. Keeping it purely professional. He's probably married with kids, anyway."

"I didn't see a ring on his finger," Sue said, smiling.

"Wow. You're observant. I'll tell him you're smitten when I see him next."

Sue jumped up. "No—don't tell him that! Anyway, I'm not. I just think he's a nice guy."

After Gina won a coin toss to decide who picked the film to watch, she chose *A Perfect Murder* with Michael Douglas. She loved horror and psychological thrillers, but she didn't choose horror, knowing Sue hated those films. At least Sue hadn't got to pick, otherwise she'd be stuck with a boring romance.

As the end credits rolled, Gina showed Sue to the front door, yawning as she stepped out into the clear, warm air.

"Lovely night, isn't it?" Sue said.

"It is."

Then Gina spun around. Tracy was standing outside her door, puffing a cigarette and wearing a lime-coloured nightgown with a grey cardigan.

"Sue, I'm glad I caught you," she said. "Next Sunday afternoon I'm having a barbeque. You want to come along?"

Gina and Sue exchanged a look.

"Erm, no thank you," Sue said.

"Come on, Sue," Tracy said. "Everyone in the village is coming. Well, nearly everyone."

Gina eyed Tracy suspiciously. Her eyes watered as the smoke wandered in her face. She faked a smile for Sue. "You should go. You'll enjoy yourself."

Gina grinned at Tracy, whose face dropped. She gave Gina a scornful look.

"I'll think about it," Sue said.

"You do that." Tracy stubbed out her cigarette and went back indoors.

"You really think I should go?" Sue said.

"Of course. If you want to."

"Strange time to ask," Sue said. "Eleven at night."

"Like it was planned?" Gina chuckled before yawning again. "Anyway, you go if you want. Really. Just because I don't get along with her doesn't mean you have to be her enemy as well."

"I'll think about it. And let me know if you want me to come with you to Dr Southwell next time. You know, for support."

"I'm not seeing him again for about a month. He really loved Toby, and I felt comfortable enough having my little treasure with me. However, I'd love you to come along. You're still my best and only friend, and I love your company."

"What about the detective? He likes you." Sue grinned.

"Like he would come to the psychiatrist with me. Anyway, I'm giving you the chance to see Dr Southwell again. I saw the way you looked at him last time." Gina gave Sue a cheeky wink and laughed.

CHAPTER SIXTEEN

That Sunday came, and Sue sent Gina a text saying she was going to Tracy's barbeque that afternoon. Gina replied, telling Sue she should go if she wanted to, and not to worry about her.

Meanwhile, Gina occupied herself dusting around the house. She was doing the dining room when she heard laughter and high voices next door. It was too hot to have the back door closed. She tried to ignore the laughter, but couldn't, so stopped what she was doing and stood in the doorway. It sounded like the whole village was there apart from her, just as Tracy had said. Gina wondered how Sue was getting along. Who was she talking to? What was being said by those jumbled voices outside? Gina had told her friend to go, that it didn't bother her, but she feared Tracy or another neighbour would try to warn Sue away from her. Sue was her only real friend in the village, but Gina knew how convincing Tracy could be. She could be very overpowering with her words, and didn't give in easily.

Gina looked at Toby lying on the grass in front of the back fence. He seemed so peaceful, not responding to anything next door.

Her throat felt dry. She filled a cup with water, but immediately chucked it down the sink. Instead, she poured a glass of wine and took it to the living room. She tapped her fingers on the side of the chair and her foot on the floor, as if she was listening to music. She just wanted the barbeque to be over.

***

The next day, Gina got a call from Amanda Sullivan, requesting an appointment. Amanda lived a few houses away; Gina was well aware that she was on friendly terms with Tracy, but she reluctantly made an appointment for that afternoon, out of curiosity more than anything else.

Amanda showed up on time, and Gina led her into the living room. She was a few years younger than Gina, shorter, but with a similar build and short brown hair. She also had a nose ring, which Gina didn't find attractive.

"I guess you're surprised to see me?" Her voice was deep, and Gina smelled cigarettes on her breath.

"Well... Yes. I don't seem to be popular in this village."

"I'll be honest with you," Amanda said. "I wasn't keen on you at first. There were all these rumours about you. You did stuff here—you know, illegal stuff. Then I was told you killed Annie. I know none of it's true!" she added quickly before Gina could retaliate.

"What makes you think none of it's true?" Gina said. "I thought her next door would've convinced you. That's where all these rumours are coming from, isn't it?"

"I will admit Tracy can be very convincing. But I chatted with Sue at Tracy's barbeque, and she told me you were a decent woman and not to believe all the rumours. So instead of listening to other people, I thought, why not find out for myself? Sue also told me about how good she feels when you massage her, so here I am."

"I appreciate that," Gina said. "Any particular area you want me to focus on?"

"I'm trying to give up smoking, but I find it impossible. I just feel tense and irritable. I thought this might help to relax me a little."

"Well, let's see. You'll probably need a few sessions, though."

Gina massaged Amanda for about forty minutes before Amanda got up, wiped off the excess oil, sat on the sofa and sighed. "Sue was right. I do feel better. Where did you learn that?"

"I took a course on it," Gina said. "I got a job at a clinic, worked there for about three years. I had to give it up when I had my breakdown. It's something I found I could do, so I thought I'd do it from home."

"I feel like I want to sleep," Amanda said.

"I'll make you a coffee, wake you up a bit."

"No, no. I'm fine really. I need to get home, actually."

"Oh… Okay. I understand." Gina faked a smile.

She watched Amanda walk slowly away down the road. *Don't believe the rumours, eh?* she thought, remembering what Tracy had said at the diner. *"She puts something in their drink after the massage session."*

***

She didn't expect to hear from Amanda again so soon, but she called the next day, asking for another appointment. Gina booked her the following Wednesday. It was the same as the last time: full-body massage with oil.

Amanda sat on the sofa afterwards. She again complemented Gina on a job well done.

"Would you like a coffee?"

Gina expected her to say no again.

"I'd love one. Milk, two sugars, thank you."

Gina stared at Amanda, not moving.

"Something wrong?"

"No… Course not. Coming right up. Do you want to watch me? Make sure I don't put any drugs in there?" Gina laughed.

But while she waited for the kettle to boil, she realised her mistake. She didn't want more grief from Tracy finding out she'd overheard the conversation in the diner.

"What made you say that?" Amanda said, taking her coffee.

"Apparently I massage people, then give them an illegal drug that makes them kill themselves."

"Where did you hear that?"

Gina had to think quickly. "I overheard it… when I was out with Toby. I didn't take any notice; people say all sorts of wild stuff."

"People like to spread gossip, don't they?"

"I know one person who does."

Realisation dawned on Amanda's face. "I bet you thought I believed that rumour when I refused a drink last week."

"Well, yes. I did wonder," Gina said. "I don't think a drug in someone's drink could make that person suicidal, though. You'd have to take a large amount."

"Would have thought so."

"I know I haven't helped myself by having contact with Annie the same day as her accident, or whatever happened."

"Innocent until proven guilty," Amanda said. "I know you're innocent. I wouldn't be sitting here if I didn't."

Gina got up and embraced her. "Thank you. That means so much to me. I thought I was hated by everyone in this village—apart from Sue, of course. She's been wonderful to me."

"I will admit," Amanda said, "when Tracy said all that stuff about you, she convinced me you were dangerous to be around. But like I said, I spoke to Sue and she told me it was all talk and I should judge for myself. I'm so glad I did."

Gina lay in bed that night thinking she'd made another friend. Amanda was nice and seemed genuine. She owed Sue a big thank you for convincing Amanda to judge for herself instead of listening to Tracy, which everyone else in the village seemed to have done. If only the other neighbours were like that, because the village itself was fine. It was in a remote area with fields to view out of her bedroom window, instead of other houses and roads like you get on housing estates. Gina loved it.

Toby snuggled up next to her, and she grinned as his fur tickled her face.

CHAPTER SEVENTEEN

After her alarm went off at seven, she made a coffee and sat in the living room, pondering what she was going to do that day. She had no clients and didn't need or want to go out, apart from for Toby's walk. Then she noticed one of her fairy ornaments had been turned on the mantel. She sighed and got up, disturbing Toby, and turned it the right way.

Tucked behind the fairy was a tiny clear bag containing some kind of white powder.

Gina stared at it and went into a daydream.

She was brought round by a sudden hammering on the door. She wasn't expecting a parcel, and her postman never came before nine, so she glanced through a small crack in the curtains. Four uniformed police officers were standing behind DI Kene.

Gina realised what was happening, and stared at what she had in her hand. She threw off her slippers and raced upstairs as quickly as possible.

Another fist hammered on the door.

She went to the spare room and opened a window. "What on earth do you want at this time of the morning, Inspector?" she called down.

"Open the door, Miss Wilkinson. We have a warrant to search your premises."

"Why? What are you looking for?"

"Just open the door, Miss Wilkinson. I'll give you thirty seconds!"

She shut the window and ran to her wardrobe. Quickly, she slid her dresses, blouses and bottoms along the hanging rail and put a nail file down a small gap in the right-hand corner of the base. She inched out a block of wood and put the bag in a small square compartment: a concealed hiding place for valuable items such as expensive jewellery. Then she rearranged her dressing gown—it had come undone in the panic—and went downstairs, where the insistent knocking continued.

She opened the door, yawning.

Kene thrust a piece of paper in her hand and entered.

Gina read the warrant. "What on earth are you looking for?" She knew the answer but had to act totally innocent. She tried to look shocked.

"We've had information that you are in possession of illegal drugs."

"Who from?" Gina was right in Kene's face.

Kene smirked. "We have our contacts, Miss Wilkinson."

She looked towards Tracy's house. *I know exactly who your contact is,* she thought. "First I'm being questioned for murder, now I'm a drug user?"

"Takes all sorts, Miss Wilkinson. Maybe you don't take the drugs yourself but give them to other people. Like Mrs Spencer and Mr Atkins."

Gina rolled her eyes. She picked up Toby, gave Kene a sharp, nasty look and then went back upstairs, following the officers who had already gone up to begin their search. Her heart was racing, and she had knots in her stomach.

She stood helpless as a policeman emptied the cupboard under the bathroom sink, then went to her bedroom, where a female officer was pulling the covers off the bed and looking under the pillows. She took the sheets and duvet cover off, then nudged Gina out of the way and shone a torch under the bed. The woman was obviously determined to search in every nook and cranny she could find in and around Gina's bed.

"I hope you're going to tidy up this mess after you find nothing," Gina said.

The policewoman ignored her.

Toby nestled up to Gina's chest, but her heart was pounding like crazy. She grew even more tense as the policewoman rifled through her dressing table, feeling around the heart-shaped mirror, chucking bits and pieces on the mattress. Gina's blood started to boil as she saw the mess her room was now in.

The officer then moved to the wardrobe, and Gina found it difficult to control her breathing. The woman searched through her hanging clothes, feeling her way through dresses and trousers, then crouched down and ran her fingers along the bottom of the wardrobe.

Gina froze, holding her breath as the woman's fingers approached the tiny crack of the secret compartment.

Then the policewoman stood up, turned to Gina and stared for a few seconds.

"Nice dresses," she said, and walked out.

Gina closed her eyes and took a long, silent breath.

She went downstairs, relieved—but had to close her eyes again when she walked into the kitchen. She counted to ten before she opened them again. All the cupboards had been turned out. Plates, cups, cutlery, saucepans, frying pans and all her cleaning products from under the sink covered the worktop and some of the floor.

"Nothing upstairs, sir," the policewoman told Kene.

"Search the living room," he ordered.

Gina just stood there and scowled at him. "You break anything, you pay for it!" she yelled.

She went to the living room and looked on, helpless, as they emptied the drawer under the TV cabinet, removed her cushion covers and piled her books on the floor. "Be careful with those!"

The policeman frowned at her as he continued to move her ornaments.

Toby wriggled in Gina's arms, so she put him down and he trotted into the garden.

"Satisfied?" she said to Kene. "You can now put everything back in its place, just as you found it."

Kene gave a small chuckle. "Sorry, Miss Wilkinson, we're very busy people. We don't have time."

Gina bit her lip. "Don't have time?" she yelled. "You found the time to come here and trash the place looking for something I never had!"

"Just doing our job," Kene said.

She was right in his face, arms folded. "Well, you're not very good at it, are you? You've dragged me down your stupid station late at night, accused me of God knows what, and then you waltz into my home and ransack it, only to find nothing! You've found no evidence against me whatsoever."

Kene just sighed; Gina at least had the satisfaction of knowing he couldn't think of any response.

She turned and, before she walked away, chuckled. "What gets me," she said, "is you've done all this on the word of my neighbours, or one particular neighbour. This is police harassment, Inspector. Get out of my sight!"

Kene walked towards the door. "I know we haven't found any evidence, Miss Wilkinson. But I think you're somehow involved in the deaths of Mrs Spencer and Mr Atkins. I don't know how, but I'm quite sure you are."

He walked out, and Gina slammed the door.

CHAPTER EIGHTEEN

The living room was a mess. Gina put her head in her hands, and Toby jumped on her lap and nestled himself against her. She cuddled him and buried her face in his fur.

"Why, Toby? Why is this happening to us?"

She got up, stepped over some scattered folders, and made her way to the kitchen to take her medication. Toby went and sat by the front door.

"I could do with some fresh air, clear my head," she said to him.

Toby jumped with excitement when she got his lead, and he nearly pulled her arm out of its socket running to the gate.

"I'm surprised you're still around here," Tracy said, as Gina passed her house.

Gina bit her tongue.

"You know, getting another visit from our friendly police."

Gina's eyes narrowed. "You must live a boring life. You spend so much of it poking your nose into other people's."

"I'm protecting my friends and fellow neighbours. It's my duty, isn't it?" Tracy smirked and studied her fingernails, covered in bright-red varnish, then walked towards the flower bed separating the two gardens. "We need to get rid of the poison in our community."

Gina walked nearer to the flower bed; they were now inches apart. "That's why you made the call and got others to do the same?"

"Like I said, it's my duty and the duty of the other neighbours to stay safe and clear the poison from our village." Tracy turned and headed back to her front door.

"I'm going nowhere! They didn't find anything!" Gina said. "The only poison around here is you and what spews out your mouth."

"Your luck will run out, dear. That's a promise."

Tracy disappeared.

Gina stood there, breathing heavily, until Toby pulled her arm impatiently.

***

After they'd walked a lap of the park, Gina sat on a bench to enjoy the August sunshine. A light breeze blew through her hair as Toby did his usual sniffing around. She heard someone come up behind her, and jerked her head round.

"Oh, Detective Carter! You startled me! What am I supposed to have done now?"

He chuckled, and her eyes darted towards him. "I'm glad you find it amusing. Please go away."

"I don't," Carter said, and sat down next to her.

Gina had to admit she liked the scent of his aftershave.

"Kene thinks you're involved in illegal activity. Actually, he's convinced you are."

"More like an obsession. What kind of policeman is he?" Her arm got pulled as Toby ran towards another dog; she held him back.

"Well, he's always been like that. You just need to be careful, that's all."

Gina's voice started to rise. "There's no evidence I've done anything."

"I know it's difficult, but try to keep calm."

"Calm!" She stood up and faced him. "Do you know what they did to my house?"

Carter put his hands up in front of her. "Take it easy."

"No, I won't!" she yelled, knocking his hand out of the way. "I don't give a damn who can hear me! I *want* them to hear me! People need to know the incompetence of our so-called wonderful, hard-working police force. When I got up this morning, my house was neat and tidy. Now it's like a nuclear bomb hit it. They trashed it, accusing me of having drugs, and yet they found nothing!" Breathless, she sat back down, and spotted an old man staring at her. "Did you hear all that?"

"You need to calm down," Carter said. "You're doing no good yelling. It won't change anything."

"Why can't people just leave me alone?"

Carter put his arm around her. Although she was fully aware that this was inappropriate, she felt the comfort and didn't resist. "Now that they've searched your house and come up empty-handed, Kene will back off. He'll have to."

"He told me they got calls saying I've got illegal drugs. It was her next door, I know it was—she practically admitted it to me when I walked out the door. And she got others to call as well. I didn't think they searched someone's property based on a few busybody calls?"

"Depends," Carter said. "You know Kene's had his suspicions of you for a while now but found little or no evidence. He gets frustrated when that happens." Gina tutted and shook her head. "Normally it takes a bit of time to get a search warrant. But when he heard you possibly had illegal drugs in your house, he called his friend who's a judge and got a warrant within the hour.

"Not only did we get told about the drugs, we also got told that over the past week or so you've had people coming in and out of your home. Word got around that you give sex and deal in drugs."

"Who's been giving you that crap?" Gina bellowed. "I know one person, maybe two, but who else?"

"They were anonymous calls," he said. "But you've been under suspicion for some time now. I can't say who is spreading this stuff, because I don't know."

"We both know it's her next door. She probably got her wrinkly old friend Eileen involved, and a few other neighbours."

What I'd really like to know is whether Amanda planted that bag, she thought. But the last thing she wanted was more awkward questions.

"Maybe," Carter said. "However, like everything else, there's no proof. No one gave their name."

"I'm not a prostitute or a drug dealer. All this is happening to me because her next door has a grudge against me. I had nothing to do with what happened to her family in the past. The only mistake I made was asking Colin if he wanted a massage—though I have to stress it was totally innocent. She really hates me. Hates the way I look and the way I dress. As far as she's concerned, if you have blonde hair, you're out being a tart and trying to steal other women's men."

"How do you know she thinks all that?"

"I keep my ear to the ground, Detective. The crazy bitch is trying to push me out. Either by getting me arrested and put away or by making my life hell so that I move. I know she has a few neighbours wrapped around her finger, and they're not the only ones."

"What do you mean?" Carter said.

"I get the feeling that Tracy and Kene talk a lot. She's got him hooked, and every time something happens, she reels him in and puts him at my door. I mean, he's an inspector. Isn't he supposed to sit in his office and let people like you go out and about?"

There was a glimmer of amusement in Carter's eyes. "He doesn't like many people; he's difficult to get along with. He says your name keeps cropping up, that's why this is happening. And yes, I know what you mean, but he likes to go out himself sometimes. Most of the time, he does sit in his office and we do the investigating outside. But there are times when he likes to do the hands-on investigating himself. I don't know why, and I don't ask. Between you and me, though, he's taken a liking to Mrs Harper. They do talk a lot."

"I know they talk a lot. She spends a great deal of her time in her front garden, and when she talks, the whole village can hear."

"Just try to keep your head down, and don't give her any fuel to ignite on you."

"I'm not going to stop what I'm doing. I'm not giving either of them the satisfaction. Though he might be disappointed he didn't find anything, I knew Kene enjoyed what he did this morning. I saw it in his face. I'm going to carry on as I have been, and no one is going to stop me."

CHAPTER NINETEEN

When she got back home, Gina went to her wardrobe and took out the small bag of powder. She sat on her bed and stared at it; she couldn't help but wonder what it would be like. Would it make her feel better? Give her that boost she so desperately needed? Her prescribed medication worked to an extent, but this… this might make her feel like a new woman.

Just try some. What harm could one tiny bit on your finger do?

She was about to open the bag when there was a knock at the door. Toby leapt off the bed and ran downstairs, and she shoved the bag back in the small hidden compartment. Another knock came, and a loud voice.

"Gina! Gina, it's Sue. Are you alright?"

Gina gave a sigh of relief and went downstairs, opened the door and flung her arms around Sue.

Sue's mouth dropped open when she saw the state of the place. "Oh my God, Gina! Your lovely tidy house! What's happened?"

She led Gina into the living room and sat her down.

Over the next few minutes, Gina told Sue the whole story of the police's search for the drugs.

Eventually, she said, "I… need to tell you something. I found a small bag of cocaine—or it may have been heroin, I'm not really sure—behind my fairy doll yesterday. Someone planted it there."

"Show me," Sue said.

Gina led Sue upstairs to her bedroom. She had never told anyone about the hidden compartment, not even Sue—but Sue had been her best friend for a year, a good listener and a comfort. Gina felt she could totally trust her.

She opened up the hidden compartment and handed Sue the small, clear bag.

Sue put her hand to her mouth. "Why would anyone do a thing like that? Do you know who?"

"I think it was Amanda. Though I'm not totally sure."

"I thought you said she was nice. Why would she plant drugs on you?"

"I don't know. Maybe this whole thing is a setup. Amanda befriends me, starts coming to have massage sessions all of a sudden…"

"You think Tracy put her up to this?" Sue said. "I… heard the two of you talking earlier."

"It's the kind of thing she'd do. She's got this village community wrapped around her finger. I know I blame her whenever something happens, but she's gunning for me. Did you hear her say my luck will run out?"

"Yes," Sue said. "I know Tracy doesn't like you, but even she wouldn't go that far. She's all talk."

"She would, you know. She's getting some kind of revenge for what happened with Karen and her father. She can't take revenge on Karen, so she's taking it out on me instead."

"I just can't see Tracy or Amanda doing something like that. It's just not like them. Where would they get the stuff?"

"Who knows what kind of people they associate with?" Gina shrugged. "Who else, then?" She went right up to Sue. "You don't think I did this, do you?"

"Oh… No. Course not." Sue gave a nervous chuckle.

Gina grabbed Sue's arm. "Look at me, Sue! Do you think I put that there myself then put the blame on someone else?" Her eyes welled up. "Do you honestly think I'm so messed up I'm taking this stuff?" Gina gritted her teeth and shook Sue lightly.

"No, I don't," Sue said; she sounded more convincing this time. She removed Gina's hands from her shoulders and hugged her tight. "Come on, I'll help you tidy up."

They started tidying the kitchen, living room and dining room, then moved upstairs. While Sue was sorting the bathroom out, Gina went into her bedroom to put the tiny bag away.

"Very small, isn't it?" Sue said over her shoulder.

"Yeah. However, there are people out there who'd commit murder for even that much. I met Detective Carter at the park this morning... Well, he kind of snuck up on me."

"I think he's sweet on you," Sue said.

Gina's eyes darted in Sue's direction. "What makes you think that?!"

"I've seen the way he looks at you sometimes. I'm surprised he hasn't asked for one of your massage treatments."

"He's been investigating me, Sue. Can't mix business with pleasure. It would land him in trouble, especially with Inspector Kene."

"I guess so," Sue said. "That's one guy you do need to steer clear of."

"Don't I know it," Gina said. "I've heard him talk to her next door. So different to the way he talks to me."

"What do you mean?"

"He's gentler. And there's a softer tone in *her* voice as well. She's got him hooked like the others."

"Here, let me get rid of that," Sue said.

Gina hadn't realised she was still holding the bag; she handed it over. "I wish I could just…"

"Just what?"

Gina hesitated. "Finish the tidying so I can relax."

"We're almost done," Sue said.

Gina watched her friend go into the bathroom, and closed her eyes when she heard the toilet flush.

You should've taken it when you had the chance.

Too late now.

You could've felt fantastic, on top of the world.

Shut up! Gina gently smacked the side of her head.

CHAPTER TWENTY

1979

Gina arrived in court with Lynda and her husband, Jake. She held Lynda's hand tight and didn't want to let go—and clung to her even harder when she saw Karen. Karen smiled at her, but Gina just turned her face away.

A lady wearing a black robe and a white wig came and tried to take Gina by the hand. Gina resisted at first, looking up at Lynda for reassurance.

"Go with the lady—you'll be fine," she said.

Gina held the lady's hand and they went into the courtroom; the two of them stood in front of a huge wooden desk with a giant carved coat of arms above it.

The judge walked in. He was in his fifties, wearing a red robe, white wig and octagonal glasses. He smiled at Gina. "How old are you?"

"I'm ten," Gina said.

"Well, now that you're ten years old, you can choose which mum you want to be with. You understand?"

Gina nodded.

"Would you tell me which mum you'd like to be with?"

"The mum I'm with now." Gina spoke without hesitation.

"Are you sure?"

She nodded vigorously.

"Very well," the judge said.

"I don't want to see the *other* mum. Ever!"

"You don't have to. She can't force you to do anything now."

When the Wilkinsons and Karen were told, Karen stormed out.

Lynda and Jake hugged Gina, who resisted at first—she'd never been hugged before—but eventually hugged them back.

CHAPTER TWENTY-ONE

Toby shadowed Gina as she paced around the kitchen. She looked at her phone for the time; it had just gone ten. She tapped her fingers on the kitchen table, pondering.

Her mind was made up.

She bent down, gave Toby a stroke and a kiss. "I won't be long."

He walked away from her. She headed to the door, but then turned back and looked again at Toby, his cute little eyes staring back. She put his lead on and headed out of the door.

She heard faint singing as they approached the churchyard. The service had started. Gina thought about turning back—she hadn't been inside a church since her mum Lynda passed some sixteen years ago—but no, she couldn't. Something was pushing her to go in. She couldn't put her finger on why, but she wanted to go inside.

She had to go in there.

She picked Toby up and slowly walked up the path, then stopped at the big wooden door. Her heart was thumping. She took a deep breath, pulled the door open and walked in just as the singing finished, glad to find an empty pew at the back. She put Toby beside her and he lay down, resting his head on her lap. As the reverend at the front said some prayers, Gina bowed her head slightly, but wasn't taking anything in. She looked around surreptitiously while the vicar talked. The wooden floor looked old and uneven. Jesus was on the cross just behind where the reverend stood. It looked similar to what she remembered, but with one big difference: no one had any hymn books or service books. Instead, there were four big TV screens on either side of the congregation, and words appeared on them during the next hymn. This was one hymn Gina didn't know, and she didn't want to sing anyway, so she kept her mouth shut.

Instead, she studied the congregation. Tracy was in the first pew on the left, next to Eileen and another woman Gina didn't recognise. Sue was on the same side as Gina, three rows down, with Amanda just behind. Almost everyone from the village was there. Gina recognised them from her walks but didn't know their names.

The words of the hymn on the screens disappeared, the singing stopped and everyone sat down. As yet, no one had seen Gina sitting at the back on her own.

However, that didn't last. When Tracy went to sit down after taking communion, she locked eyes with Gina. She scowled, her mouth open. Expressionless, Gina just sat there. Sue also spotted her, and looked surprised when Gina smiled at her and Amanda; there was no reaction from Amanda. Gina shook her head, sighed and gazed at the floor. She was slightly relieved that no one had spotted Toby yet. However, she knew she couldn't keep him hidden.

Gina remained where she was, her head down, as everyone filtered out of the back. She felt eyes on her and could hear whispers.

"This is a nice surprise."

Gina looked up, though she already knew who it was. Sue's calming, gentle voice couldn't be mistaken.

Sue stared for a moment when she saw Toby. "I'm not sure how the reverend would feel having a dog in the church."

Gina resisted the urge to roll her eyes. "He's an assistance dog—I can take him anywhere and no one can stop me. Did I not explain this to you, Sue?" Gina couldn't help it; she felt frustration rip through her.

Sue looked startled for a moment, then smiled and said, "Coming out to the hall? They serve coffee, tea, cakes and biscuits."

Gina sat there deliberating for a few seconds. "Sure, okay." She was pleased Sue didn't continue to argue the fact. But when they got to the door leading to the extension hall in the back, Gina stopped.

"It'll be fine," Sue said, and pulled Gina through the door—carefully, as Gina was holding Toby—to a space near the back of the hall. "Wait here. I'll get the coffees."

Gina looked around the hall. People were standing in small groups, chatting among themselves. Amanda was with Tracy and Eileen. All three spotted her, and Tracy came strolling over.

"I'm surprised to see you here," she said. "You must be in a great deal of pain."

Gina looked puzzled. "Why must I be in pain?"

"Because I know when the Devil enters the house of God, it's very painful. You'll be asked to leave, anyway; disgusting rodents are not allowed in this church."

Tracy strode back to Eileen and Amanda, leaving Gina to hold in her fury. The moment Tracy started talking, they all stared in Gina's direction. She shook her head and looked away, not surprised at all she was the subject of their conversation.

She was desperate to talk to Amanda, mainly to see if there was any change in Amanda's attitude towards her. However, it didn't seem like a great idea at that moment; Tracy was no doubt spewing gossip about her.

A couple of women went over to Tracy and pulled her away. Eileen went with them, leaving Amanda by herself. This was Gina's chance. Hesitantly, she started to walk towards Amanda—but a cheery voice called out and the vicar stepped in front of her, blocking her way. He was slightly taller than Gina and not much older, with brown hair. He was in his grey robe with a white dog collar.

"Reverend, how are you?"

"I'm fine, thank you." He stopped and stared at Toby.

Gina knew what was coming, so she did her usual explanation speech on assistance dogs.

The reverend seemed a little unsure, but accepted it. "I must say, it's very nice to see you here. Don't think I've ever seen you in our church."

"You haven't," Gina said. "I haven't been in a church since my mum passed away."

"Well done for making that step. I've heard you've been having some difficult times of late?"

Gina looked in Amanda's direction. She was still by herself.

"Er, yes. But I'm fine, really," she said.

"You can talk to me any time—my door's always open. Allow God to lead you down the right path."

"Thank you, Reverend, I…" Gina stopped. "The right path? What do you mean? You believe this stuff that's being said about me?"

For a moment, he stood and said nothing. Then: "Excuse me, Gina." He walked away.

Gina stood there, her blood boiling, then sat at a table against the wall.

"Everything alright?" Sue handed Gina her coffee. "You look like you want to murder someone."

Gina shot a look at her.

"You know what I mean. It was just a figure of speech. I meant you look angry."

"The reverend believes all the gossip about me. Told me that God will put me on the right path. You'd have thought he of all people would believe in me."

"Reverend Duncan? He's alright. I've been doing some voluntary work for him. I was considering asking you to help out too, actually, but you never come here—apart from today—and also Tracy is one of his main helpers. She's always in and out of here."

"That explains his comment. She's got the reverend in the palm of her hand, then?" Gina took a sip of her coffee. "I'm so glad she hasn't convinced you. You're practically the only friend I have." Gina gently stroked Toby, trying to calm herself.

"Not that she hasn't tried. She's pulled me aside quite a few times and warned me about you," Sue said.

"I bet she has. I wanted to talk to Amanda, but…" It was too late. Tracy and Eileen were back with her. "She hasn't contacted me since, you know, the raid. Not even a text."

"I wouldn't talk to her here. Not about that, anyway," Sue said. "Try calling her later, or send a text."

"I really wanted to talk to her—you know, in a casual setting. After she had a session, she would ask for another one, then another. Then the last time she came was when I found the drugs behind the ornament and I got raided. I haven't heard from her since."

"I know how it looks," Sue said. "But you don't want to go throwing accusations around."

"Oh, I wasn't going to straight-out accuse her. Just talk to her, and kind of slip in what happened. I want to see how she reacts. It's niggling away at me."

"You had three other people that day, including me. For all you know, I could've put it there."

They both chuckled.

Gina again saw her chance. Tracy was talking to the reverend, and Eileen had wandered off. This time, Gina took it.

"Hey, Amanda." Gina felt an adrenaline rush.

"Oh, Gina. I'm… surprised to see you here."

Gina eyed her suspiciously.

"Never seen you in here. I heard what happened— hope you're alright?"

"Apparently, the police got some calls saying I had drugs in my house—but they didn't find anything. The thing is, Amanda, before the police arrived, I found a small bag of powder behind my fairy ornament. I wonder who put that there?" Unblinking, she leant in closer to Amanda. "They'll pay if I find out who it was!"

Amanda stepped back, and Gina thought she saw fear in her face. "Sorry, Gina, but I have to go. Lots to do."

"Call me if you want another session," Gina said.

Amanda ignored her and went back to Tracy.

"What did she say?" Sue said, when Gina returned to their table.

Gina took a mouthful of coffee. "I think she did it. Did you see how nervous she seemed?"

"Yes, she did look a bit twitchy, but maybe she thought you were outright accusing her."

"I didn't say anything of the sort. She brought it up, and I told her what happened." Gina munched through her third chocolate digestive without realising it.

"You looked angry at her just before she walked off," Sue said. "What did you say?"

"We were just chatting. I don't think I said anything nasty."

"Then why does Tracy keep scowling at us? She looks furious."

"She always looks like that," Gina said, and laughed.

She wasn't laughing for long when she saw Tracy marching towards her.

"You got a nerve, don't you?"

Gina glanced at Sue, then back at Tracy. She didn't say anything.

"Not only do you come inside the house of God, but you make threats?"

"Gina?" Sue tugged on Gina's arm.

"Who have I threatened?" Gina said.

"You threatened Amanda. Who has been very nice to you lately."

Sue gaped at Gina.

"We just talked," Gina said. "I don't remember making any threatening comments." She looked around. "If I can find her, we can sort this out."

"She's gone home," Tracy said. "Very upset she was, almost in tears."

Gina looked at Sue again. "You don't believe her, do you, Sue?"

"I'm sure it's a misunderstanding," Sue said.

"Amanda told me you found drugs behind your fairy ornament," Tracy said. "You accused her of planting them there. I knew it—I knew you had drugs—but to have the nerve to accuse someone of planting them? Then making threats? Just goes to show what kind of a person you really are."

Gina turned to Sue, looking for support, but Sue just shrugged.

"I did find the bag behind my ornament, but I didn't put it there," Gina said. "I wouldn't know where to get that sort of thing. And I don't remember making threats to Amanda."

"You liar," Tracy said. "You told her whoever put that bag behind your ornament or whatever is going to pay. She said your face changed and your voice was different. You really scared her. But you don't scare me. The only one that's going to pay around here is you!" She poked Gina hard in the chest, then turned to Sue. "Why are you friends with such trash?"

She stalked out, muttering and shaking her head.

"Come on, Gina," Sue said. "Let's go home."

Gina followed Sue out of the church. "Did you really say that to Amanda?" Sue said, as they crossed the road.

"I never said anything threatening."

"So you never said whoever planted those drugs is going to pay?"

"No. I wouldn't say something like that. Come on, Sue, you know I wouldn't."

Sue sighed. "Are you sure... this isn't one of those moments where you say something then can't remember you said it?"

Gina looked around. "Come inside."

They both went into the house; Gina took off Toby's lead and Sue followed her into the kitchen.

"You haven't told anyone about that, have you?" Gina said.

"No, of course not." Sue looked surprised. "I would never tell anyone personal information you tell me." She put her hand on Gina's and gave a wry smile. "I just wonder if sometimes, when you're stressed or angry, you blurt stuff out without realising what you're saying."

"Then completely blank out and can't remember I said it?"

"Well, yeah. Something like that."

"So, I'm a crazy woman, then?"

"I never said that."

CHAPTER TWENTY-TWO

After Sue had left, Gina called Amanda straight away. The ringtone lasted a long time before a voice answered.

"Yes?"

"Oh, hi, Amanda." Gina sounded flustered. "I just wanted to apologise for the misunderstanding."

"Misunderstanding?" Amanda said. "You accused me of planting drugs in your house, then calling the police on you!"

"No, I didn't mean to actually accuse you—but someone did put a small bag of what looked like drugs behind my fairy ornament. Then my house got searched. Sometimes I do overthink, maybe, I don't know…"

"Well, I have to say there's one thing I know, Gina."

"What's that?"

"I know I've made a terrible mistake."

Gina smiled. "That's alright, I've made tons myself."

"I mean I made a mistake in not listening to Tracy when she constantly warned me about you."

Gina's smile dropped into a frown. "So, she's sucked you in too, has she?"

"She hasn't sucked anyone in, Gina. She kept telling me what you were like and to be on my guard. I didn't listen. I wanted to know for myself what kind of person you were, and now I'm seeing clearly. It wasn't me who planted those drugs, but I know who did."

"Okay. Are you going to tell me?" Gina felt palpitations in her chest.

"Come on, Gina, stop playing your stupid little game. We both know it was you that put that bag there.

You're just looking for someone to pin it on, and here I am. Obviously you've found out about my past."

Gina was quiet for a few seconds; her mind was everywhere. "What do you mean, I put it there? And what past? I…"

"You know what I mean," Amanda said.

Gina stroked Toby, who'd jumped up and perched himself beside her. "First of all, Amanda…" Her voice was now sharp. "Why on earth would I put drugs behind my own ornament? I suppose you think it was me who called the police, too, asking them to search my own house, being that I'm so crazy. And for your information, I know it was Tracy who called the police. She practically admitted it. If I'd put those drugs there myself, how would she know to call them? And I was told other neighbours reported me as well. Explain that one!"

Amanda went quiet. "Well, it wasn't me who put it there. However, I think Tracy was right about you."

Gina sighed. "So you believe what she says about me, then?"

"I didn't at first. You seemed harmless, and really friendly. But I'm not so sure now. You accuse me of planting drugs in your house, then threaten me—in a church, of all places. I can see why you don't have any friends."

Gina tried to think back to the conversation they'd had in the church hall, but her mind was blank. "I didn't threaten you. You're making that up."

"You said if you find out who planted those drugs, they're going to pay. I know when I'm being threatened, and with Annie and that guy who died…"

"I don't remember saying that to you."

"Well, you definitely did. You scared me, actually. I don't feel safe around you."

"So you actually think I gave Annie and that Atkins guy—who tried to rape me, by the way—drugs that somehow made them take their own lives? Maybe you're the one who's crazy!"

"It's a possibility, Gina. Drugs can do all kinds of things to people. I should know—I used to take… Well, you know all about it."

"How could I know about anything you used to do or take?" Gina started to breathe heavily.

"Maybe from that detective—what's his name?"

"Who, Kene?" Gina said.

"No, the other one. Carter, I think that's him. Did you enjoy hearing about my past, Gina? About when I was in my late teens and someone I trusted got me into drugs. I was young and weak and took on board everything they said. It took me over three years to get cleaned up, after I got arrested for possession. I had to agree to rehab and strict therapy to stay out of prison. I bet he enjoyed telling you all that—after you slept with him, of course."

Gina just sat there listening to Amanda talk and talk. Her head was pounding so much; she just wanted Amanda to go away. "Amanda, I *didn't* know all that about you, and I don't remember threatening you, either. Whether you believe me or not is up to you, because I don't care at this point. Bye!" She hung up.

Not even a minute had gone by before she got a text from Amanda telling her to delete her number and never contact her again. Gina did just that, then put her phone down, closed her eyes and carried on stroking Toby.

Amanda had been sucked in by Tracy and her web of lies. Maybe the two of them had concocted this little plan. Amanda had seemed to be nice to Gina in a way no one else really was, apart from Sue. Could this have been her plan all along? Suddenly asking for massage sessions after Tracy's barbeque…

She went over what she thought had really happened in her head. However, she kept losing her train of thought, so she got her notebook and pen and wrote it down.

Amanda, who used to be on drugs, had befriended Gina to the point where Gina would trust her. She then got hold of the stuff somehow, through her contact or whatever, and planted it behind Gina's ornament when Gina left her alone in the living room. Then the police were called for a search.

Gina smiled as she continued writing. *Their plan was for me to get caught in possession of drugs, get me put away, then Tracy would've succeeded in getting me out of the village. But it didn't work, thanks to the secret compartment in my wardrobe. I asked Amanda about it in the church hall. She went on the defensive, denied everything and got upset in the process, and said I threatened her. I don't remember saying anything threatening. She thinks I'm sleeping with Detective Carter. No surprise there.*

Gina put her pen down and read what she'd written. It sounded crazy, but the more she read and thought about it, the more she was convinced. Tracy and Amanda had planned the whole thing.

CHAPTER TWENTY-THREE

Gina gulped down some wine, then sent a text to Sue asking if she'd come over. Sue was on her doorstep within thirty seconds.

"How much have you had?" Sue asked after they hugged.

"Only a couple of glasses. You want some?"

"Go on then, just one. Did you talk to Amanda?"

"Oh yeah," Gina said. "Some friend she turned out to be. She's convinced I deliberately accused her of planting the drugs." Sue raised her eyebrows. "I just told her that it was there; I wasn't saying she put it there. I didn't mean for it to come off that way." She downed another glass of wine in one swoop. "She got really upset. Told me that because she was on drugs years ago, I must have convinced myself she'd put it there. I didn't even know she was on drugs. Did you?"

"No, I didn't," Sue said. "Quite shocking, really. I'm also shocked she would tell you something like that about her past."

"She thought I knew. She was convinced I checked up on her and found out about it."

"How would you check up on something like that?"

"The usual—she's convinced I'm sleeping with DS Carter. No doubt she's been brainwashed by that fat cow next door. And then she told me never to contact her again."

Sue shook her head. "I don't know what to say."

"Don't say anything, Sue. To hell with the lot of them. I don't care what they think of me. They're all trash as far as I'm concerned, and they can all rot." Gina poured herself more wine. "I think it was all planned, anyway; it just didn't work out for them. The only one around here who I can call a real friend is you."

"Gina, I think you've had enough of that." Sue reached for the bottle.

"I'm fine!" Gina's voice was sharp.

Sue nodded. "You said it was all planned. *What* was all planned?"

"I wrote it down."

Gina found her notebook and told Sue what she thought about Tracy and Amanda's plan to get rid of her. Sue shook her head when Gina had finished reading.

"I know it sounds crazy," Gina said. "I thought so too, but the more times I read it over, the more convinced I became that it might be true. The police were supposed to find that tiny bag, and if they had, I wouldn't be sitting here right now."

"That's true," Sue said. "You'd have lost everything. Your home. Toby."

Toby went up to Sue and sniffed her foot. She just looked down at him and smiled.

"You don't like dogs, do you, Sue?"

Sue looked at her in surprise. "I'm not that keen on them, no. One bit me when I was little, and I've never really liked them since."

"Toby would never bite you. Look how small and cute he is." Gina picked him up and hugged him tight. "This gorgeous little chap is my absolute world. He looks after me, always lying by my side when I'm struggling or having a bad day. He's the best therapy I ever get."

Gina's phone rang, and she put Toby down. There was no name, but she recognised the number.

"Hello, Detective. What can I do for you? And before you say anything, I can assure you I've been a good girl. I haven't poisoned anyone or tried to push anyone out the window."

Carter chuckled. "I know that. I was just wondering if I could pop by and see you tomorrow?"

"Erm… tomorrow? What for?" Gina looked at Sue, who just shrugged.

"I'm off duty and I haven't seen you in a while, so I thought I'd come by and see how you're doing—maybe have a chat or go for a walk, experience one of your massages?"

"I'm not sure…"

Sue shrugged again and mouthed "Why not?" at her.

"Look. You're not under any investigation or going to be questioned about anything. I can come in the morning so your neighbours don't think anything dodgy is going on."

Doesn't matter. They're already convinced of that anyway. "Oh, alright. See you tomorrow, then."

As she hung up, Sue smiled. "Well, that Detective Carter has certainly taken a shine to you."

"What do you mean?" Gina felt herself blushing. "I'm not going down that road. I made that mistake with…"

"Your psychiatrist?"

"Yeah. That went alright for a while, then the last six months of it were so stressful. I'm better off on my own in that sense."

"Have you told anyone else about that, besides me?"

"No way," Gina said. "Who on earth would I tell that to?"

"I don't know. Amanda? Carter?"

"No, I haven't. Especially Amanda. We weren't that friendly, and I didn't trust her totally—you know, one hundred percent. I hadn't really thought about it, anyway. It's the past now."

"Let me know how it goes." Sue gave Gina a wink.

"Nothing's going to happen. Can you imagine the gossip around here? It's bad enough now."

"Got nothing to lose, then."

CHAPTER
TWENTY-FOUR

The next morning soon rolled around. Gina put on a tiny bit of makeup, a thin, dusky-pink jumper and light-blue leggings.

Carter arrived at about half past ten. He wasn't in the usual suit he wore on duty, but casual dark-blue jogging bottoms and a grey jacket. Gina checked up and down the road before letting him in.

"It's a free country," Carter said. "You can see whoever you like."

Gina smiled. "I know. Most of them have made up their minds about what goes on here anyway. It's become boring, actually. I guess I can't control their thinking, so I shouldn't care so much."

"That's right," Carter said. "Just live your life and try to put your neighbours out of your mind."

"Yeah. It's just very difficult when you get dragged down the station late at night, being accused of murder. When your house gets ransacked because your neighbours assume so much and talk so much. I get that her next door is angry for what Karen did to her family…" Gina sighed and looked at the floor. "She's taking that situation out on me, like she's getting some kind of revenge."

Carter walked closer to her. "That's what it is." He gently lifted her face. "She doesn't really believe this stuff about you; it's just in her head and she thinks it bothers you. Just try to show her you don't care what she or anybody thinks. You know what you're doing, that should be good enough."

"You said she was friendly with your inspector?"

"Yes, it does look that way. But Kene wasn't happy about not finding anything in the search here. I overheard him say those that reported it wasted police time. He hates that. That won't happen again, I can assure you."

Then Carter cupped her face and leant in without warning.

She pulled away when their lips had barely touched.

Silence filled the room. They couldn't look at each other.

"How about that wonderful massage I keep hearing about?" he asked eventually. "I could do with it; police work can be really stressful." He smiled at her.

"Yeah... sure." Gina's nerves were on edge. Though she trusted Carter totally, she hadn't massaged a man since that day with Jim Atkins.

She set everything up, put on soft music and massaged him for about thirty minutes. When she was finished, she went to make two coffees while he got dressed.

"Well, I can see why your neighbour Mrs Houldsworth says you're the best massage therapist on the planet," he said when she returned.

She laughed, nearly spilling the drinks. "I doubt that. I bet there are people in this world much better than me. But thank you anyway. You did need it."

"Like I said, police work is stressful, and it's been a tough few weeks. Maybe I need more than one session?"

"Yeah, maybe," she said. "I'm very up and down at the moment, too. I never had a happy childhood, thanks to my natural mother. It seems to have followed me into my adult life. Anyway, I'm going to try and get on with my own life and not worry about anyone else."

"Your natural mother messed you up that bad?"

"You have no idea. She never left me alone, even after I turned ten and I was officially adopted."

Toby jumped on her lap and nestled himself against her.

"How did that come about?" Carter asked. "The adoption, I mean?"

Gina's breathing became heavy.

"It's alright," Carter said, and put his arm around her. "Don't talk about it if it upsets you."

He slowly turned her face to his and their lips gently touched. Gina started to open her mouth and she felt his tongue on hers. A tingle rose in her body. Then she saw Tracy's face flash in her mind. She pulled away quickly.

"I'm sorry," she said. "I'm really sorry. I can't do this."

"I thought you weren't going to worry about your neighbours," Carter said. "I just wanted to kiss you." He wiped a tear away from her cheek.

He stood up, but Gina didn't let go of his hand. She pulled him back down to the sofa.

"You're right. I wasn't going to worry about them, was I?" she said. His eyes lit up and a smile started to form. "I don't care any more. I don't care what they think of me, I'm going to do what I want. To hell with them!"

"That's good. Keep thinking like that." Carter put his arms around her and gave her another soft, gentle kiss. He brushed her blonde hair back with his hand, and they kissed more passionately.

"Thank you," he said, when they broke apart. "That was wonderful."

He took his coat off, took her by the hand and stood up again—but she pulled him back, kissed him and said, "Here."

CHAPTER TWENTY-FIVE

1979

Three months had passed since Gina stood in court to choose which parent she wanted to be with. She hadn't heard from Karen in that time, which made her happy. However, the fear lingered in her mind: Karen was still out there and could grab her any time she wanted.

The fear became real when Lynda opened the front door to find presents on her doorstep, gift-wrapped in plain pink paper. Gina knew who they were from. She told Lynda to throw them in the bin.

Gina got off the bus and walked towards the school gates—then stopped dead. Karen was standing near the entrance. Gina had no doubt it was her. Children walked past her, but she didn't move.

Eventually, she walked away, and Gina slowly went in.

Gina hated school. She liked the teachers, but the children in the playground would come up to her and say things like, "Your mum is up at that window with a gun and she's going to shoot you." They'd run off laughing, leaving Gina looking at the window, shaking with fear.

When it was time to go home, Gina asked her friend Leanne if she could walk to the bus stop with her. However, as they approached the stop, Gina froze. Karen, smiling, was waiting for her. Leanne tried to tell Gina it would be alright, but Gina wouldn't move.

Karen walked up to them. "Why are you so afraid of me, Gina? I thought we might ride on the bus together, or I can take you shopping. I'll treat you to some nice toys and buy you sweets."

Gina shook her head and started to cry. Leanne took Gina's hand and led her onto the bus. She sat down but could still see Karen from the corner of her eye; she desperately wanted the bus to move.

When she got home she ran, crying, into Lynda's arms.

***

Over the next few nights, Gina would wake up screaming. She wouldn't eat properly or leave the house.

At the weekends, she would spend time with her dad, Jake; she didn't see him much during the week, as he worked long hours in a warehouse.

One Saturday—after Gina had been off school for two weeks because she was still refusing to leave the house—Lynda told her they had to go shopping. Reluctantly, she went, clinging tightly to her mum.

They were in Asda when Gina froze again.

"What's the matter?" Lynda said.

"She's in here."

Lynda and Jake both scanned up and down the aisle, but saw no sign of Karen.

"She's not in here," Lynda said. "I think it's your mind playing tricks."

Gina shook her head. "I know she's here. I can't see her, but I know she's here."

Her parents both held her hands and they continued shopping. But when they got to the till, Lynda spotted Karen putting her shopping on the conveyor belt.

"How did you know?" Lynda said.

"I just knew. I… had that feeling."

***

The following Monday, Gina was due to return to school. She was crying all morning, not wanting to go—and when her mum got her outside, she clung to a lamp-post, screaming and screaming. Lynda had no choice but to take Gina indoors and keep her at home for another day.

CHAPTER TWENTY-SIX

Gina let Toby out into the back garden and went for a shower. She stood with the water beating against her while she pondered over what had just happened.

I've done what the neighbours have accused me of doing.

As she sponged herself down, she smiled at the thought of what her neighbours—well, one neighbour in particular—would say about it. Gina was sure Tracy would have seen Carter arrive or leave, because Tracy rarely missed a trick. If she heard a car door shut, she'd be at her window like a hungry wolf waiting for its prey. Also, she'd be extra interested, as Carter had come in his street clothes and his own car, not the unmarked police BMW he normally arrived in.

Well, there was nothing she could do about it now.

***

The next morning, Gina stepped out with Toby; he dashed for the gate, pulling her arm off as she shut the door. Sue was leaving her house at the same time.

Then a distinct voice bellowed, "Have fun with the detective?"

Gina took a breath and faced her. "Yes, I did, thank you." She turned back to start walking.

"Let me guess," Tracy said. "You gave him a massage, then took him upstairs, right?"

"Not quite. I gave him a massage, but I didn't take him upstairs."

"Liar." Tracy sounded furious. "Everyone knows what you are, and they're sick of it."

Gina's medication had settled inside her, and she decided to take Carter's advice on board. "I didn't take him upstairs, I swear."

Tracy sighed and shook her head.

"We did it on my sofa." Gina had a big grin on her face. She looked Tracy up and down. "You don't have any kids, do you?"

Tracy took a step back. "What's that got to do with you?"

"Nothing, nothing at all," Gina said. "But I'm not surprised. I mean, how often do you and Colin have romantic times together?"

"That's none of your goddamn business!" Tracy's voice dropped to a growl.

Gina nodded. "That's what I thought. Especially with the rumours about you." She tutted and shook her head.

"What rumours? What are you talking about? I see what you're trying to do, but it's not going to... Will you shut up, you stupid mutt!" Tracy screamed at an impatient Toby.

Gina scowled at her, then blew a kiss down at Toby. "I'm not trying anything. It's just what I heard."

"Who from?"

Gina smirked.

"I've not done anything wrong," Tracy said. "And as for me and my husband, we're just fine. You're not getting your dirty hands on him."

"I don't intend to," Gina said. "You can keep your robot."

Colin came out. Tracy went over and whispered something to him, making sure Gina couldn't hear.

"Obey your commands, Colin!" Gina yelled as they both turned to go inside. "Just like a robot."

Gina set off again on her walk. Sue, who had been standing with her mouth open as she watched the proceedings, came over to join her. They walked slowly up the village road, with Toby sniffing at every wall.

"Was that necessary?" Sue said.

"It's how I feel. She's giving me enough of her mouth. I thought giving some back wouldn't hurt."

"You shouldn't give her fuel like that. Especially about Carter. She'll be calling everyone in the village, telling them you're sleeping with your clients."

"Doesn't she accuse me of doing that anyway? She's so sure I do it, what difference does it make?"

"You *told* her you did it," Sue said. "And with Detective Carter as well. You shouldn't make up stuff like that."

Gina lowered her head, then looked up at Sue, guilt written all over her face.

Sue's eyes were like saucers. "You mean you *didn't* make it up?"

"It just happened," Gina said. "Don't ask me how—it just did. I can't even remember how it started." She started to grin, and relaxed even more when Sue's shocked face joined her in a grin of its own. "I actually did what she and her cronies accused me of. And I don't feel one ounce of guilt. I don't care."

"Well, good for you," Sue said. "You did it on the sofa, then?"

Gina nodded.

"I didn't hear you!"

"I'm not that loud!" Gina burst out laughing, and they carried on with their walk.

When they got back about twenty minutes later, Tracy was back outside, this time with Eileen. Gina grinned at them as she walked up her garden path.

A croaky voice echoed behind her. "You're disgusting!"

"I know," she said without looking back. She just went inside and shut the door.

***

A week went by with no real dramas, although Gina saw Tracy most mornings when she took Toby for his walks. Tracy would make comments at her, but Gina chose to ignore rather than retaliate. She didn't go outside the village; she got all she needed from the village store, and otherwise just sat at home doing her diamond painting and crochet.

Today, though, she had arranged to go on an outing to the Canterbury Wildlife Park with Sue. It was Sue's idea, and it had taken some convincing to get Gina to go.

"Come on, let's have a nice day out," Sue had said. "We're in the second week of September, so the kids are back at school. It shouldn't be crowded."

"I'd really like to go," Gina said. "It's just been a long time—and I can't leave Toby all day long, so he'll have to come with us."

"Take him on his walk before we go. He'll be fine. You can't take him to a zoo—they won't let him in."

"An assistance dog can go anywhere. I've told you many times."

"But even an assistance dog might distress the other animals. Gina, I know you do really want to go. You just have to get through that nervous stage. Take some medication with you in case you get panicky, and I'll be with you the whole time. Please, Gina, leave him here. He'll be fine just this once."

Gina sighed, but agreed. "I can't be more than six hours."

"That's plenty of time," Sue said.

Gina woke that morning after a restless night; she'd only properly dropped off two hours earlier. She did her normal routine, taking extra meds than usual. When she got back from Toby's walk, she put some anxiety pills in her bag and picked up Toby, cuddling him and saying she wouldn't be too long. He gave her a scornful look, which didn't make her feel any better. She put down some fresh food and water. He barked like mad at the knock on the door.

Gina bent down and showered him with kisses before they left. She kept looking back as they walked towards the bus stop at the end of the village.

"He'll be fine," Sue said.

At the park, they spent just over four hours looking at every animal they could find, and Gina was tired by the time they made it to the gift shop. She treated herself to a giant meerkat, a pin badge and a fridge magnet, and bought Sue another pin badge to go with the charity shop smiley-face badge, as well as a medium-size lemur. Sue thanked her and hugged her, but said she shouldn't have bought her the lemur—it was expensive.

"Well, I'm so glad you talked me into coming here. I've had the time of my life today," Gina said. "I just loved those meerkats; I could've watched them forever. They're cute, unlike some of the others."

"You couldn't stroke or give kisses to those wild dogs," Sue said.

Gina chuckled. "No way. I'll stick with my gorgeous Toby. Can't wait to see him; he's never been alone for this long."

On the bus back to the village, Gina sat with her eyes closed while Sue was on the phone to her mum.

Sue gave a big sigh when she hung up.

"What's wrong?" Gina asked.

"Mum's in pain and wants me to go over there. She keeps forgetting to take her tablets. You'll be fine walking up the village?"

"Yeah, course I will," Gina said, realising she didn't have much choice. "I hope she's alright."

They got off the bus, hugged each other and went their separate ways. Gina trudged up the village as quickly as she could with her meerkat under her arm, ready to relax and cuddle up to Toby. She could barely pick up her feet as she walked up her garden path.

"Toby!" she called, eager to let him know she was back while she fumbled for her keys in her bag. "I'm home, sweetheart."

Nothing. No response.

She tapped the door. Still no bark.

That was odd. Whenever anyone came to the door, no matter who it was, Toby would always bark like mad.

She dropped the keys as her hand started shaking. She scooped them up, forced the key in the door and turned it, her weariness overpowered by sudden panic.

Gina pushed the door, which stopped with a bump. Her heart pounded as she pushed harder, squeezing herself through the gap—and there was Toby, lying motionless against the door.

CHAPTER
TWENTY-SEVEN

She dropped everything she was holding and knelt beside him. He looked so still. She stroked him gently, willing herself to stay calm, but the knot in her stomach got tighter.

He… he just decided to sleep. He's fine, there's no way he's gone, she told herself.

She put her hand on him, checking for breath; she couldn't feel any. Then she put her head to his chest, listening for a heartbeat. She thought she heard a slight thudding.

You're fine, you're fine.

HE'S DEAD! a voice boomed inside her head.

"No, *no*! You're *not*!" she said out loud. "You're… You're just not well, that's all." She stroked him again. "I'll get you down the vet's, baby."

Her shaking hand fumbled in her bag for her phone. She called the vet's for an emergency appointment; they told her to get there ASAP.

She wrapped Toby in a blanket while waiting for the taxi. It arrived in just over five minutes, though for Gina it seemed like hours. She picked Toby up carefully in her arms and took him outside. The light had started to fade; the wind blew and dark clouds gathered as she carried him to the taxi. The taxi driver, a big middle-aged man with a bushy beard, got out and opened the door. Gina got in the back. She took deep breaths, trying to stay as calm as she could.

"The vet's—quickly as possible, please!"

They drove off.

Gina leant over, looking out of the front windscreen. "You need to hurry. Please!"

"Look, lady, I can't break the speed limit," the taxi driver said. He sounded Italian.

They approached some traffic lights—which changed to red, and she felt the force of the brakes being applied.

"Oh, come on, come on!" she yelled.

"I can't go through red lights, lady. This isn't an ambulance. I'm going as fast as I can."

Gina sat back and closed her eyes. *You're going to be okay, you're going to be just fine,* she kept telling herself, over and over. Tears burned the back of her eyes.

The taxi pulled up outside the vet's surgery. "That'll be seven pounds thirty-seven."

Gina threw him a tenner and told him to keep the change. She struggled to get out and shut the door with the side of her arm.

She was about to go around to the main entrance when a side door opened and two young nurses came towards her.

"Are you Miss Wilkinson?" one of them said.

"Yes," replied Gina.

They took Toby in the side door, Gina right behind them. They went straight into a small room and put him on the table. There was no movement from him. The vet, a stocky grey-haired man, soon came in and placed a stethoscope on Toby's chest, checking for signs of life. Gina studied his face; there was no reaction. Without a word, he took Toby through to the back, going out of sight. Gina anxiously leant over the table to see where he'd gone.

She stood waiting. Her foot was bouncing, and she tapped her fingers on the table.

About ten minutes later, the vet came back. Toby wasn't with him. There was a sombre look on his face as he met her anxious gaze; he didn't have to say anything.

She put her hand over her mouth, started shaking. Tears streamed down her face.

"I'm sorry," he said.

Gina had her head down. The young nurse sat her down, putting a consoling hand on her arm.

"He was healthy," Gina sobbed. "When I left him this morning, he was absolutely fine. He can't be gone, he just can't be! I don't understand." She looked up at the vet. "You're mistaken—he was just sleeping, that's all. I'll take him home. He'll wake up soon and be as right as rain."

The vet didn't move. "I'm so sorry," he said. "I'm afraid he really has gone." His voice was low and sombre.

"He was such a healthy little dog, how can he just…"

"We could do an autopsy. It would cost, though."

Gina didn't raise her head to look at him. "I don't care! Whatever it costs. I need to know what happened! He was my baby, my poor baby."

"It'll take a few days, maybe a week," he said. "We'll call you when we get the results."

She nodded and was led out through the back by the nurse.

"Can I get you anything?" the nurse asked.

Gina, still crying, shook her head. "The only thing I want is my baby back. He's my assistance dog. What am I going to do?"

The nurse rubbed her back, not really knowing what to say except, "I'm sorry."

"I just want to go," Gina said.

The nurse opened the back door, and Gina trudged out into the rain.

She wandered through the town, not knowing what direction she was going. Shutters were coming down in shops. Gina folded her arms across her chest; her shirt was stuck to her skin, though she was wearing a bra.

The last place she wanted to go was back home; opening the front door with no Toby would be unbearable. She sat on an empty bench in the town centre. The strong breeze was making her shiver, but she didn't care. She just sat there with flashes of Toby stuck in her mind—and that image of him lying in front of the door with no movement. He was an active, healthy, energetic little dog who'd made Gina feel better in her lowest moments. The pain ripped through her body, as if she'd been slashed with a sword. She hadn't felt like this since her mum had passed.

Gina heard someone approach her.

"Are you alright, luv?"

She raised her head and found herself looking into the eyes of a wrinkly old woman in a grey coat. Gina said nothing, just nodded. The woman went to say something else, but Gina raised her hand to stop her. Finally, the woman left her and carried on.

She began to shiver more as the wind grew stronger. Someone else approached—a man, this time—and she kept her head down.

"What are you doing, sat here like this?"

Gina jerked her head up immediately.

"You look frozen." DS Carter was standing tall over her with his long brown coat on.

He bent down and rubbed her hands. Gina's eyes welled up, and Carter pulled her to her feet and embraced her. That was all it took. She sobbed in his arms, and he held her tight, asking her what was wrong. She had tear stains down her face. He walked her to his car and put her inside.

She was glad to feel the warmth of the heater but laid her head back against the headrest and couldn't look at him.

"What's wrong?" he asked again.

Gina tried to tell him, but the words just wouldn't come out. She knew if she forced them, she would just burst into tears again. "Toby…" Tears burned her eyes. She put her hand to her mouth as if she was going to be sick.

"Something wrong with Toby?" Carter asked. "Is he ill?"

Her breathing was getting heavier and she was starting to gag. Still she didn't look at him, but she felt her head being turned gently.

Gina took longer breaths, with a lot of sniffing. "Toby… is…" She couldn't finish.

"I'll take you home."

"No! No, please, I don't want to go back home. I can't walk in that door without him there, barking and jumping up at me. I… I just can't."

"We can't have you wandering the streets at this time. You need to go somewhere. Anywhere else you can go?"

Gina shook her head.

"We'll just sit here for a bit, then."

After about twenty minutes of consoling her, Carter drove Gina home. This was the part she was dreading the most.

"I don't want to go in there," she said. "I just can't face an empty house. He was always there to greet me if I hadn't taken him out. Barking when he heard me put the key in the door, jumping up at me when I entered, and I'd pick him up and cuddle him. He was adorable. When we did go out together, he helped me to cope with being out on my own." Gina tensed her whole body, fighting her urge to cry. "Can I stay at your place for a while?"

Carter looked at her. "I'm afraid not. I live in a flat near the station. If anyone found out you were staying, it would cause problems."

"Why would it cause problems? It'll only be for a couple of days, and I won't be any trouble. I know I'll have to go home eventually, but right now, so soon, it's just unbearable." Gina had desperation in her voice, but when she looked into his eyes, she knew he was going to say no.

"You've become known to the police," he said. "I know it's through no fault of your own and you've done nothing wrong, but it would be very unwise for you to be seen coming out of my flat."

"So that's it," she said. "They all think I'm a criminal, though there's no evidence against me."

"They don't think that. It's Kene, mainly."

"What's wrong with him now? What else am I have supposed to have done?"

"Nothing," he said. "He found out that I visited you off duty. He knew I was there for some time and thinks there's something going on between us."

"How does he know about that?"

"Apparently, he got a phone call. So I heard, anyway."

Gina sighed; she knew the second he said 'phone call'. "I should've known." She shook her head. "She just can't help herself, can she? Okay, she knew you were there in your causal clothes and made her judgement, but why take the trouble to phone your inspector just to tell him? Aren't you free to see who you like off duty?"

"Well, yes," he said. "However, like I said, you've come under suspicion, and while there's no evidence against you, it's clear he doesn't like you. He still thinks you could've been involved with what's happened. He told me seeing you on a personal level could damage my career, and I'm looking for promotion."

Gina put her head in her hands. "Why did you bring me home, then? You should have just left me on that bench."

"I saw the state you were in," Carter said. "I wasn't just going to leave you like that."

Gina unclicked her seat belt and opened the door.

"Do you want me to come in with you?" he asked.

"No. That's okay. I must do it alone. I don't want to get you into more trouble. Thanks for everything you've done."

CHAPTER
TWENTY-EIGHT

Gina walked slowly towards her front door and put the key in. By now, Toby would usually be barking and squealing with excitement. But there was just silence—an eerie silence that sliced through her like a butcher's knife. She entered into darkness and stood with her back against the door, shaking, as she heard Carter drive off.

Gina turned on the passage light, then the living-room lights. Her eyes went straight to Toby's bed—his small, round, light-brown bed with bone shapes imprinted around the outside. She stared at it, putting her hand over her mouth, fighting the urge to cry.

She went to the kitchen and took some tablets. There, her eyes went to Toby's dinner mat—personalised, with "Toby" printed on it—and bowl. Gina stared. She couldn't help it; it was like she'd been put in some sort of trance.

Gina desperately wanted to call Sue and tell her what had happened, but just saying the words out loud would set her off again. She grabbed her phone and sat there staring at it, at Sue's name. Finally, she pressed the call button. It rang for a good minute before Sue answered.

"Hello?"

Gina didn't speak at first.

"Hello! Gina? Is that you?"

"Yes," Gina said. "I know it's late, but can you come over?"

"I can't now, love, I'm still at my mum's. I'm going to stay with her for a few days. She had a fall. She's alright, but it frightened her and she's a bit frail." Gina's heart sank, and Sue asked, "Is something wrong?"

"It's Toby. He's… he's gone. I found him by the…"

"Sorry, Gina, I've got to go—she's calling me. If you're feeling unwell, why don't you take some tablets and snuggle up in bed with Toby? I'll come and see you in a few days."

"Well, it's…."

The phone went dead.

Gina tried not to get upset, but she just couldn't help it. She totally understood that Sue had to look after her mum, but she had no one else to turn to. And Sue telling her to snuggle up with Toby—that set her off big time.

Her mouth felt dry. She went to the drinks cabinet in the dining room and drank some whisky from the bottle. In the corner, on the shelf, was his high-vis lead with its ASSISTANCE DOG label. She stared at it for some time.

What if he'd been with me?

An awful sensation went through Gina. She wanted to know what happened; she just had to know, even if it was the last thing she did on earth.

She went upstairs to get into her nightgown, taking the whisky bottle with her and swigging a mouthful now and then.

Gina got into bed and lay there with her mind in maximum overdrive. What had happened to Toby, and why? She just couldn't understand it. He hadn't seemed unwell when she'd left him. Something wasn't right—he was too young and healthy to just go like that.

She lay there for a couple of hours, trying to get some sleep, but she just couldn't. She felt completely alone. She wanted an end to this pain and suffering. Most of all, she wanted to be with Toby, her little baby, her bundle of joy, who made her feel better at her lowest. Better than any psychiatrist or counsellor.

Gina got up, went downstairs and took her medication out of the cupboard. One by one, she lined her tablets up along the kitchen table, then got a bottle of vodka and a shot glass. Although she desperately wanted to find out what had happened, it wouldn't bring Toby back. She would never see him again—and the thought of ending the pain she was in overpowered the need to find out how he died. She just wanted to slip away quietly.

Gina poured vodka into the shot glass as tears streamed down her face. She drank it in one swoop, then topped up the glass and placed it in front of the tablets. She made sure all the lights in her dining room and living room were off, keeping only the passage lights on.

She stood there, staring at her kitchen table. What had she got left in life? Sure, there was her best friend, but Sue was friends with everyone in the village, and she had her mother to take care of.

Gina took a deep breath. She felt at peace with herself. She was scared, yes, but she kept thinking about Toby, how she desperately wanted to be with him. She was sure she was doing the right thing.

CHAPTER
TWENTY-NINE

1985

As Gina got out of the car that had brought her home from school, there was a police car outside her house. What was going on? Had something happened to Karen? Had she done something?

The last time she'd seen Karen was two days ago; she'd been in the supermarket again when Lynda and Gina were there. This time, they'd come face to face. Karen had tried to speak to Gina, but Lynda had ordered her away.

In the six years that had passed since the adoption, Karen had never left Gina alone. Whenever Gina arrived at school, Karen was at the gate and would stare at her through the window. Whenever she got out of the car, she had to meet a teacher to escort her inside, even though she was now sixteen and in her final year.

Gina took a deep breath and went inside the house. Lynda was sitting in her chair, crying. Two police officers—a man and a woman—were present.

Gina froze.

There was an eerie silence for a few seconds.

The policewoman approached Gina, but Lynda stepped in. "No, I'll tell her."

"Tell me what?" Gina's voice was sharp.

"Your father had an accident at work."

Gina dropped to her knees. She knew the outcome right away.

Jake worked in a warehouse at the paper mill. Apparently, he'd been walking down one of the aisles when a forklift backed out after putting a pallet full of paper on the rack. It hadn't lowered the forks enough, and pulled the pallet off. It fell on top of Jake Wilkinson, killing him instantly.

***

The funeral took place two weeks later. As Jake's coffin was lowered, Gina and Lynda stood together, sobbing, at the front of the crowd gathered around the grave—until Gina jerked her head up and started to shake.

"No, no... She's here."

"Who? Karen?" Lynda said. "I can't see her—where is she?"

Gina pointed. And there was Karen, standing at the back.

Lynda stormed over to her.

Gina stayed put and watched an angry Lynda talking to Karen, poking her in the chest; she sobbed more, knowing this was not the time for such a scene.

But then Karen and Lynda started walking towards her. Gasping, she backed away, but Lynda put her arm around her.

"She wants to tell you something. It's alright."

Karen swallowed. "Sorry about your dad. I'll leave you alone. You won't hear from me again."

She walked off and disappeared.

CHAPTER THIRTY

Gina put the first tablet in her mouth and washed it down with a shot of vodka, then poured another and picked up the next tablet. However, as she went to take it, Toby flashed through her mind. He was standing in a field, staring at her, smiling.

She threw the tablet on the table and chucked the vodka down the sink.

She had to know what had happened to him—how he had died so suddenly. He couldn't have died on his own; someone did something to him. They got in the house somehow when she was out with Sue.

Gina went into the living room and looked at the photo of herself and Toby together. It was as if he had told her not to do the thing she'd planned.

She took three Valium, washing them down with water this time, went to bed, and finally dropped off to sleep.

**

When Gina's alarm went off, she turned it off, rolled over and closed her eyes again. She didn't want to move or do anything all day. There seemed no point in taking a shower or getting dressed; she had no breakfast or lunch—just one coffee all day, and her dose of tablets. All she could do was lie in bed with her phone in her hand, waiting for it to ring with news on Toby's autopsy. The day seemed like weeks, and she hadn't heard from Sue all day. However, she kind of understood that, as

Sue was busy looking after her mum. Life for Gina seemed worthless right now. She didn't want to do anything but curl up and sleep forever.

For the next two days, Gina remained in her bed, getting up only when she had to. She drifted in and out of sleep, but that was due to the alcohol she drank, mainly in the afternoons. She forced herself to eat some lightly buttered toast when her stomach got crampy. Her phone was by her side at all times, waiting for that call. Often she was tempted to call them to find out whether they'd done the autopsy yet—but she realised that wouldn't make it go any faster.

In the late afternoon on that second day in bed, her phone finally went off. She sat up quickly, knocking her glass off the bedside table in her haste to grab the phone.

Her heart sank when Sue's name appeared on the screen.

She answered, but couldn't get any words out.

"Hello, Gina—are you there?" Sue said.

"Y…yes. I'm here." Gina's disappointment started to build up. "How's your mum?"

"She's feeling better, thanks. It wasn't serious. I should be home tomorrow. I just rang to see how you are. Are you feeling better? You sound better than the other day."

"Yeah, a bit," Gina lied.

"I'll pop around tomorrow when I get home. Take care."

Gina looked at herself in her heart-shaped mirror. Her hair was sticking out from all ends and her eyes were puffy, but she just couldn't get herself moving to do anything about it. She picked up her glass and poured some more wine, the last bit she had beside her bed. She'd gulped it down and taken a long breath when her phone went off again. She didn't rush for it this time, thinking it was Sue calling back, or someone else, until she recognised the vet's number.

"Yes?" she said quickly.

"Miss Wilkinson?" replied a man's deep voice.

"Yes, speaking," she said, impatient.

"It's about your dog, Toby. I've done the autopsy you requested. It seems... Well, it seems he died of poisoning."

"Poisoning? What are you talking about?" Gina hiccuped and put her hand to her chest. "He had his normal breakfast that morning before I went out."

"Did you give him any treats as you were leaving?"

"No. I didn't." She hiccuped again but didn't pull the phone away to hide it.

"We found bits of biscuit, not quite digested. It seems he ate two biscuits just before you found him. They had poison on them. It's the only explanation."

There was silence for a dozen seconds.

"I don't understand. He hadn't had any biscuits. There must be some mistake."

"I'm sorry, Miss Wilkinson. There is no mistake. We've double-checked."

"I just don't see how it's possible he could..." Gina suddenly broke off, got out of bed and went to the front door, where she knelt and rubbed her hand over the floor. Bits of what looked like biscuit crumbs stuck to her fingers.

She could hear the vet calling her name.

"Sorry, yes, I'm here. I just had to check something. Thank you. I appreciate what you've done in such a short time."

"No problem," the vet said. "Do you want Toby cremated?"

"Yes, please, but I want his ashes."

"Okay. It'll take a few days. We'll let you know."

Gina hung up the phone and stormed into the kitchen. Her hurt and sadness had turned into blood-red fury. Her stomach churning, she bit her lip as she stood looking out of the kitchen window, her fists clenched. She thumped the draining board. It hurt.

She put on her coat and marched out of the house. She was too angry now to be scared to go out on her own, and besides, it wasn't a busy town or anything—just her local park, where she'd taken Toby on so many occasions. Stopping at her gate, she looked back at Tracy's, staring at her window as the fury rose in her body. She knew what had happened to Toby—and she knew who was responsible.

As she made her way to the park, she phoned Carter. "Can you meet me somewhere?"

"Where are you?"

"Walking towards the park."

"Okay," Carter said. "I'll meet you there in ten minutes."

At the park, to her relief, there was no one else around.

Carter pulled up in his black BMW, climbed out and gave her a hug. "What's wrong?"

It took Gina some time to say anything, she was sobbing so much in his arms.

"She poisoned my dog." She finally blurted the words out. "She killed him, my poor little Toby."

After she calmed down, Carter put her in his car. He didn't drive off anywhere—just sat there with her, a sombre look on his face.

"I can't do anything," he said. "Anything that involves you, I can't investigate or even look into."

"But you have to!" Gina said. "Who else is going to do it?"

"You can turn up at the station and report it. One of our uniformed officers will deal with it. Proving anything, though, will be difficult. Are you sure she poisoned him?"

"The vet told me he found traces of biscuit in Toby's digestive system, along with the trace of poison. It had to be her! Who else would it be?"

"It could be youths playing an evil prank. It does happen, you know."

Gina vigorously shook her head. "Nope—it was her! I just know it was!"

"Make a report to uniform, but I doubt they'll be able to do anything." Carter put his arm around her, but she pulled away from him. "I'm sorry, Gina. I know he meant a lot to you."

"Toby was my life, my baby. He always would comfort me when I needed it, was always reliable. I hate this goddamn world. If it was some human, they'd be on it in no time. But oh no, not for a dog. Drives me mad."

Carter was checking his watch.

"Sorry to keep you," she said. "I know you're busy."

"I'm sorry," he said again. "Report it, get hold of the vet's report and see what happens. You've got nothing to lose, really."

Walking home, she knew he was right.

CHAPTER THIRTY-ONE

Tracy and Sue were talking at Sue's gate. Gina slowed down to a snail's pace, willing one or both of them to stop and go back in, fighting the urge to throw herself at Tracy.

It was no good. They could be there all day—after all, it was common knowledge that Tracy could talk for England.

She walked past, looking at the ground.

They both stopped talking.

"Hey, Gina, are you alright?" Sue said.

Nodding, Gina fumbled her keys out of her bag. When she went to unlock the front door, she had to fight back tears at the silence on the other side.

"You know something, Sue?" Tracy said. "It's so nice and quiet around here lately."

Anger boiled inside Gina as she turned and saw Tracy's grin.

"Where's your little mutt, then? Abandoned you?"

She balled her hands into fists and stared unflinchingly at Tracy. She waited for her to say something else but nothing came, just a stare down. Sue was just studying the floor, giving off "I'm not getting involved in your quarrel" vibes.

Gina turned and went inside. She leant against the door and put her hand over her mouth. There was no Toby to greet her with his tail wagging like mad, no Toby to jump up at her and lick her face when she picked him up. There was nothing. Total silence.

Then there was a knock on the door.

When she opened it and saw Sue, she flung her arms around her. She tried to stop the tears coming, but it was no good.

"What on earth's wrong?" Sue asked.

"Toby's… gone," Gina sobbed.

"What do you mean 'gone'?"

"Poisoned… Someone poisoned my baby."

"What?" Sue sounded shocked. "Poisoned? How?" There was urgency in her voice, but Gina didn't answer. Sue grabbed Gina's face to look at her. "Tell me!"

Gina told Sue what had happened when she'd got home that day and found Toby lying still behind the door. She told her what the vet had said.

Sue just held her, not knowing what to say.

"They poisoned him when we were at the wildlife park."

"Who did, love? Who?" Sue said.

"That bitch next door and her wrinkly old friend."

"They wouldn't do a thing like that!"

"Everything else she's tried has failed. So she picked my weakest spot. She knew how much I loved Toby and what he meant to me."

Sue followed Gina into the front room. "I don't think she would go that far. Sure, she dislikes you a lot, but actually poisoning Toby? I don't know."

"You heard her just now. 'Oh, isn't it quiet around here lately? Where's your mutt, abandoned you?' She knew he wasn't there—she knew because *she* killed him!"

"Doesn't prove she did it, though," Sue said. "It could've been kids."

"Just like when my garden was trashed?"

"I don't know what to think," Sue said. "I will admit what she said out there wasn't nice, but you know her— she's all mouth. She'll say anything to get your back up. Where would she get poison from, anyway?"

"Weren't Eileen and her husband chemists once?"

"Yes," Sue answered. "But there's no way George would get involved in something so horrible. He's a very sweet old man—he wouldn't do anything like that, I'm sure."

Gina sighed and shook her head. "Colin seemed nice. We always got on well, had nice chats. Then came that misunderstanding at the pub that night, and now he's not the person he once was—and I'll tell you why, Sue. It's because *her* next door has him wrapped up tight. She shouts 'jump', he says 'how high?'."

"What's that got to do with George?"

Gina rolled her eyes. "Eileen's got George in the same way. Think about it, Sue—the two of them putting pressure on poor George, so much pressure he breaks. Others might be involved in it as well. Amanda, for instance. I'm determined to find out somehow!"

"How are you going to do that?" There was concern in Sue's voice.

"Don't know yet. But I can't just let it go. Toby was my companion, my whole life. I'm really struggling without him. I can't go to town on my own—when you haven't been able to go with me, I've always taken Toby. I can't do that now. And if I'd taken him to the wildlife park, this wouldn't have happened. He'd be with me right now."

"Are you blaming me, Gina?"

Gina did not meet Sue's gaze. "No, of course I'm not."

"I'd better get home," Sue said. "I've got a few things to sort out."

"Sue?" Gina put her hand on the door, stopping Sue from leaving. "We're still friends, aren't we?"

Sue didn't say anything for a few seconds. "Of course we are. Nothing's changed. Not from my perspective, anyway. You should report this to the police. Take the vet's report so you have proof, and see what they say."

"That's what Jack said."

"Jack?"

"I mean Detective Carter. But I don't see the point—I can't prove who did it, and they're not going to make a great effort, are they? To them it's… just a dog. I know they won't do anything. It's a waste of time."

"Let me know if you change your mind. I'll come with you if I can."

After Sue had gone, Gina wandered into the kitchen, taking in the silence of the house. She heard the small pitter-patter of paws following behind her and looked around, excited, but nothing was there. She leant against the sink, tapping her fingers. The urge to find out what had happened to Toby was still eating away inside her.

CHAPTER THIRTY-TWO

Checking her diary the next day, Gina saw she had an appointment with Dr Southwell in the afternoon. She didn't want to see him, and thought of cancelling. However, after her previous appointments, Gina had always found she felt better, more confident in herself. He always told her to do what she wanted, and provided it was within the law, there was nothing wrong with trying to make herself happy. She'd had some emotional appointments with Dr Southwell, her childhood being the main focus and the hardest to talk about.

She decided not to cancel, and took some extra tablets. She knew this appointment would be about Toby—and that she would have to get there on her own. No Toby to comfort and help her. She'd asked Sue, but her friend couldn't make it this time. She still felt hurt inside her chest, which got worse whenever she saw Tracy and Eileen talking just outside. Did Tracy spend her time talking outside, not inside, just in case Gina came out?

Gina walked past them with her head down.

"So quiet around here, Eileen. No stupid mutt disturbing our peace lately."

Gina stopped but didn't look back. She bit her tongue, took a tissue out of her black bag and dabbed her eyes. She heard chuckling behind her.

***

Gina managed the journey thanks to the extra Valium she took, but she was shaking when she went into Dr

Southwell's clinic. Once in his room, she sat down and looked out of the window, though it was frosted. She was still shaking, and he noticed she wasn't her normal self.

When she settled, silence filled the room. However, she heard Tracy's voice calling Toby a mutt and saying how peaceful it was.

"Need to sort that fat bitch out." Gina's voice was very low as she mumbled the words.

"Sort who out, Gina?"

There was no response.

"Gina!"

Southwell clicked his fingers at her. She jumped a little and stared at him.

"Who are you talking about? Your neighbour?"

"What? Sorry," she said.

"I take it from what you've just said that you've had more trouble from your neighbour?"

Gina frowned. "I didn't say anything."

"You said"—he gave a little cough—"'Need to sort that fat bitch out.'"

Gina shook her head. "I said that out loud?"

Southwell nodded. "Exact words. You mumbled it, but I heard every word. Was it so strong in your thoughts that the words tripped out of your mouth?"

"I don't remember saying that. Are you sure?"

"Hundred percent."

"My dog Toby was poisoned."

Gina struggled, but told Dr Southwell about all the events leading up to the day she found Toby. He didn't interrupt her once, not even when she choked back the tears or put the blame on Tracy.

"How do you actually know it was your neighbour who did this?" he asked.

"Who else would do it? If it wasn't her, then she got someone or paid someone to do it for her." Gina raised her voice. She thought highly of Dr Southwell—someone who was actually good at his job—and she hadn't expected a question like that from him.

She waited for him to speak, but he sat there looking at her, mentally examining her.

"But it might not have been her," he said eventually. Gina tutted and looked away. "You seem to have this woman locked in your mind, Gina. Anything goes wrong or something really bad happens, you assume she had something to do with it."

Gina jumped out of her chair. "Toby meant so much to me!"

Southwell didn't respond. He sat calmly, gazing up at Gina as she trembled, tears in her eyes.

"He was my baby. We bonded so well, and he always helped me when I went out on my own. And now he's gone. People say it's just a dog, get another one—well, no one's said that out loud to me yet, but I know that's what a lot of people will say. If it was a *child*, it would be all over the news."

She stopped. There was silence in the room. Her hands were balled into fists, and she sat down again, sobbing.

"He was a wonderful, gorgeous little dog," Southwell said when she seemed to have calmed down a little. "He was so well-behaved when you brought him here. What would make you feel better?"

"Just… finding out what happened. The truth of what happened, how it was planned."

"What would you do if you found out? I mean, if your neighbours were responsible, what would you do?"

"I don't know."

"Would you perhaps be so angry as to physically hurt them?"

"No. I don't think so. I'd feel like I wanted to kill them, but the thought of being put away in prison or spending my life in an institution would probably prevent me from doing anything. It's just…"

Gina played with her hands; she sighed, tutted and shook her head. She waited for Dr Southwell to say *Whatever it is, just let it out*. He looked calm and patient.

She took a deep breath.

"Some years ago, when I was eighteen, I got into trouble. I put another girl into hospital in a fight we had." She studied Dr Southwell, but his expression didn't change. She looked at the floor. "The point is, I didn't remember doing it. I went home, then soon after, the police came and arrested me. But I didn't remember hitting her or anything."

She looked up again.

Southwell's gaze moved off her and down to his notebook.

"Interesting that you've never mentioned this before," he said. She shook her head. "You were scared I'd section you, put you in an institution?"

She nodded and dabbed her eyes with her tissue. "I guess you have no choice now, do you? I shouldn't have said anything, I *knew* it!"

He smiled at her. "What I want you to do is go home, try to relax, do some of your painting or whatever it is you like to do."

"Diamond painting," she said.

"Yes. Try to relax, Gina. I know that's difficult, especially now because you're hurting so much from the loss of your dog. But that will pass in time." She glared at him, thinking he was like lots of people. *It's just a dog.* "I do understand that to some people, losing a dog or any pet you love so much can be like losing a member of your family."

Gina saw in his face that he meant what he said. She smiled through her tears.

As she got up to leave, he offered her a lift home. "I don't have any more patients today," he said.

"Yes, thank you," Gina said.

As they walked out through the reception area, Gina got a phone call; it was the vet, telling her Toby's ashes were ready. She asked Dr Southwell if he could take her there instead.

"Course I will," he said.

CHAPTER
THIRTY-THREE

Her heart pounded as they approached the entranceway. She took a deep breath and headed inside, Dr Southwell by her side. There was no one in the reception area, so she waited, tapping her fingers on the desk.

She looked behind her, to where an old man was sitting with a white fluffy Bolognese on his lap. She hurried over.

"Toby! Oh, Toby darling, there you are." Her voice was high, excited. "I thought you'd... What are you doing with my..."

The man pulled his dog away from her. "His name's Freddie."

She shook her head, then noticed Southwell looking at her calmly.

"Miss Wilkinson."

She turned. There was a nurse standing inside the doorway, holding a plastic bag; Gina recognised her from when she'd rushed Toby here on the night he died. She slowly followed her out into the corridor. The nurse gave her the bag. Gina peeked inside, and her heart sank when she saw a small silver urn. The nurse gave her a sympathetic look before she left.

On the way home, Gina looked anxiously at Dr Southwell. "Are you going to put me away for trying to take that man's dog?"

Southwell chuckled. "No, I'm not—not unless you harm yourself or are a danger to anyone else. It's clear you're very upset; your emotions are all over the place right now."

"That dog looked just like Toby," she said, trying not to cry.

She now felt empty, and didn't feel any better when she saw Tracy, Eileen and Amanda talking outside as Southwell drove towards her house. She kept her head down and got out of the car, not making eye contact with Eileen or Tracy.

"You still on for bingo, Eileen?" Tracy was saying. "I'm going to get Sue to come with us. It's about time she mixed with proper respectable ladies, instead of trash."

Gina had the urge to turn around and bite back, but she put the key in the door.

"It's so much quieter around here now that noisy little mutt's gone."

Gina went inside and slammed the door. Wiping her eyes, she heard laughter outside. She went to the living room, sat down and took the urn out of the bag.

She stared at it.

"My gorgeous little baby," she sobbed.

She sat and held the urn for a while, then placed it on her mantelpiece between her fairy figurines.

Outside, they were still laughing. They were laughing at her, the three of them, laughing at her expense. The best thing to do was ignore them, but she couldn't.

They killed your baby, now they're laughing about it, the voice in her head kept repeating.

She picked up her colouring book, but put it down again after five minutes. She tried to watch TV, but she couldn't follow anything that was on. She looked at Toby on the mantelpiece, then glanced out of the window.

Gina jumped out of her seat and peered through the net curtains with her arms folded. They were still there, chatting and laughing—but now Sue had joined them. She seemed really happy, laughing with them. Gina was going through pain and heartache, and there they were, happy and laughing. Why would Sue be laughing and joking with them?

They poisoned my baby and...

Gina walked away from the window. She thought hard and shook her head.

No. It's not possible. Sue wouldn't do that. She just wouldn't do something like that—distract me, get me out of the house, convince me to leave Toby at home so they can poison him? Sue's my friend—she's comforted me so often.

Gina wondered why these thoughts would even enter her head. She looked out of the window again; they were still there, but just chatting now. Eventually, they dispersed and Sue walked towards Gina's garden.

Gina opened the door before Sue knocked, and stared at her.

"You alright?" Sue said. "You look like you've seen a ghost."

Shaking her head, Gina came out of her trance. "Yeah, I'm fine."

They went to the kitchen.

"I just came to see how you were holding up."

Gina put the kettle on to make some coffee.

"I'll have tea, if that's alright," Sue said.

Gina spun around, and the coffee jar slipped from her hand to the floor. They both bent down to pick it up. Gina took it from Sue, turned and carried on.

"Lucky it didn't break," Sue said.

Gina said nothing. She spooned coffee into her cup with a shaking hand; some of it went on the worktop.

"Do you want me to do that?" Sue asked.

"No, it's fine." Gina knocked a spoon onto the floor and went to pick it up, but Sue grabbed her hand.

"What on earth is wrong with you, Gina? You seem really flustered."

"Just a bit out of sorts, that's all."

She tried to read Sue's eyes. The thought of Sue getting her out of the house so *they* could get to Toby wouldn't disappear. Her heart said Sue wouldn't, but her head said she would.

"Go on," Sue said. "You go and sit down; I'll make the drinks."

Gina sat in her living room, staring straight at Toby's urn. She took her coffee, but Sue held on to the cup until she had both hands tight around it.

Sue spotted the new object on the mantelpiece. "Ah, is that Toby's—"

"Ashes. Yes."

"Are you going to keep them there or scatter them?"

"I thought I'd scatter them in the back garden. He liked lying down out there. Not just yet, though. I… want him where I can see him for now."

"How did your session with Dr Southwell go?"

"Fine," Gina said. "Then I got the call from the vet to pick up the ashes. Dr Southwell took me, then he brought me home. I got the usual nasty comments from her outside."

"Take no notice." Sue chuckled as she said it. "You know what she's like."

"Did they say anything to you about me?" Gina didn't expect Sue to say yes, but the question just slipped out.

"No. They didn't mention you."

Gina studied her face, but couldn't tell whether she was being truthful.

"What did she say to you?" Sue asked.

She took a mouthful of coffee. "Gloating about Toby not being here. She also said she's going to invite you to go out with her and Eileen, to bingo or something—which is totally fine," she added quickly. "Get you to spend time with 'proper respectable ladies instead of trash'—like me."

"You know how she feels about you, so she'll say anything to get under your skin. I don't think that of you—I wouldn't be sitting here if I did. I know losing Toby has knocked you back big time, but I bet he's up there running around in a field as happy as can be. I'm always here for you, Gina. You're my best friend. Always."

Gina got up and hugged her. Tears rolled down her cheeks. "Thank you, Sue. I thought… you know?"

"You're not getting rid of me that easy. And try to ignore Tracy; she puts so much trash in her stomach, no wonder it comes out of her mouth."

Yeah, but I'm still sure she poisoned my dog.

"Why don't I come around tomorrow night?" Sue said. "We can watch a couple of films with a bottle of wine and some nibbles."

"That'll be great. Maybe do me some good."

"It'll do you the world of good. Being cooped up by yourself for too long makes you so depressed. I'm just sorry I didn't spend more time with you sooner."

They hugged, and Gina felt better.

CHAPTER THIRTY-FOUR

When Gina woke up the next morning, the lights were still on and the TV on standby. She sighed and shook her head as she climbed out of her chair, then she stamped her foot on the floor a few times to get rid of the pins and needles. She went to Toby's urn.

"Mummy's got to stop dozing off in her chair," she said.

She went upstairs for a shower but found herself wandering into the spare bedroom instead. She could see the village from there.

Gina was about to leave, undoing her dressing gown ready to step in the shower, when she caught a glimpse of Sue walking out of her gate. She wasn't expecting her to pop round at this time, but she did up her gown, ready to run down and open the door. However, Sue walked straight past and into Tracy's. This got Gina curious. The horrible thoughts came back to her... Then she remembered last night, when they'd planned their girls' night in and she'd felt she had her best friend.

She wanted to ignore her curiosity and walk away, but found herself rooted to the spot. What were they talking about? Was it about her? After all, she seemed to be Tracy's favourite subject.

Sue disappeared inside Tracy's house. Gina wanted to get in the shower, but she still didn't move.

What are they talking about? Sue's my best friend; that interfering bitch is trying to drive a wedge between us. It's fine, though—Sue knows what she's like, she won't take any notice. Sue sees the good in everyone, but even she knows Tracy talks trash.

Gina went to the bathroom, took off her gown and stared at herself in the mirror.

How can your best friend still be friendly with that woman? The woman who trashed your garden, set up the police raid in your home, murdered your precious little Toby? How do you know Sue wasn't a part of it? Distracting you, pretending to be your friend? Can you trust anyone? They murdered your dog, your loving companion.

"Shut up!" Gina yelled. She put her head in her hands. "I want this shit out of my head."

She got in the shower and started soaping herself, rubbing hard with her hands. The voices were still there. She tried to push them aside, but they were yelling. Gina continued to scrub, then she winced. Droplets of blood seeped from her thigh. She took the shower hose and turned the water to cold.

After she got out, her thigh was still bleeding and sore. She put a plaster on it, got dressed and went to the spare bedroom. She looked up and down the village again; no one around. Was Sue still in that woman's house? Was her mind being poisoned against Gina?

Silently telling herself not to be silly, she went downstairs and made herself a coffee, fighting the urge to have something stronger. She carried her cup into the living room, sat down and picked up her diamond painting. Her hand was a little shaky as she held the small tray of sparkling beads. She took deep breaths, trying to relax, but found herself staring out of the window as if her head was being turned by a giant magnet. Then another horrible thought occurred to her: she criticised Tracy and the other neighbours for looking out of their windows so much, but now she was doing the same thing.

She picked up her phone and tapped on the text symbol.

Hi Sue, just wanted to say thank you for your support last night, and I'm looking forward to our girls' movie night in.

Why can't you tell her that tonight, when she comes over? What if she doesn't come? Why wouldn't she? Because her next door has put her off, told lies? You know how persuasive she can be. Her voice is powerful.

Gina thumped her head a couple of times and pressed send.

One minute later, her phone lit up and vibrated. Gina's heart rate went up.

She's going to cancel—I just know she is.

Any time. I'll bring some snacks if you get the wine? We'll have a good evening. See you tonight.

Gina smiled and sighed with relief, giving herself a telling-off for putting herself through unnecessary worry and stress. Sue wouldn't turn her back on her.

Feeling more relaxed, she picked up her diamond painting again.

The doorbell rang.

She peeped through the net curtains to see who was standing there, thinking it might be Carter or Inspector Kene, come to accuse her of something else.

As she opened the door, she was frowning. "Amanda? What can I do for you?"

"I want to say sorry about your dog." Gina scanned Amanda's face for signs of deceit, but found none. "I know how fond you were of him. I also wanted to say sorry for... you know, what happened that day in church. It sounded like you were trying to accuse me of planting drugs in your house, and I guess I overreacted."

Gina stayed quiet. She slowly opened the door, then followed Amanda into the living room, where they both sat in a tense silence.

What does she want?

To trick you again.

No, she sounds genuine.

You stupid, naive woman.

"Do you want anything?" Gina said, breaking the awkward stalemate. "Tea, coffee, something stronger?"

"Oh, yes please. Got any wine?"

"Yes, I have." Gina walked to the door, then turned around. "You'd better come with me. I might put drugs in your glass, or you might put drugs behind my ornament." She giggled when Amanda scowled at her, and Amanda quickly laughed with her.

Gina poured two glasses of wine, and they stood against the worktop.

"Can we just forget about everything that's happened in the past?" Amanda said.

"I'm over it already. What's done is done."

"That's good," Amanda said. "What happened to Toby?"

"He was poisoned." Gina took a mouthful of wine. "Someone put biscuits through my letterbox when I was out with Sue at the wildlife park."

"Do you know who did it?"

Who's she trying to kid here? She knows. Probably helped.

"I can't prove who did it."

"You haven't reported it, then?"

"What's the point? They'll just laugh at me."

Amanda hesitated, then said, "I was wondering if we could start up the massage sessions again?"

So that's what she wanted.

I told you; she's tricking you again.

What if she likes my massages?

You saw her laughing with Tracy and Eileen.

I saw Sue laughing with them too. It doesn't mean anything.

They're all laughing at you. They're against you, like some evil conspiracy group.

"The thing is, Amanda, I'm still mourning the loss of Toby. I need to be in the right frame of mind for massage. I'm just not there right now."

"I can understand that—he was such a sweet little dog. I saw you taking him for walks; I can imagine how much you loved him."

"He was my world, Amanda. My baby."

Gina saw the disappointment in Amanda's face. She wasn't sure whether she did understand—Gina was the only village resident who owned a dog.

"Maybe in a couple of weeks I'll feel better and we can start up then," she said.

"I'll call you in a couple of weeks, then."

Gina took the empty glass and saw Amanda out.

She's not trying to befriend you.

I'm not listening.

She's trying to find out what you're thinking, how upset and angry you are about Toby. They murdered your baby; you must get revenge.

I'm just looking forward to my girls' night in with my best friend.

You stupid woman!

CHAPTER THIRTY-FIVE

Sue arrived carrying crisps and a bag of sweets.

"Still wearing your smiley-face badge, I see," Gina said.

"Yes, of course," Sue said. "Brings a shine to my life every day."

They went to the living room and scanned through the movie channels, but couldn't agree on what to watch.

"I'll toss you for it," Gina said.

"Sure, okay."

She found a coin and asked Sue to call. Sue yelled, "Heads!"

It landed on tails.

Gina scanned the films. "What about this one? *Paranormal Activity*?"

"Oh no, not horror," Sue said. Gina grinned at the fearful expression on Sue's face.

She carried on looking, reading what each film was about.

"This one," she said eventually. "I really want this one. I haven't seen it."

"*John Wick*," Sue said. "I like Keanu Reeves, but I'm not sure that one's a good idea."

Gina had a serious look on her face. "I want to watch it, Sue!"

Sue read the synopsis; Gina didn't shift her gaze from her friend's face. "A retired hitman goes after some thugs, after they killed his dog. You want to watch that after what happened to Toby?"

"Yes!" Gina's reaction didn't change. "I won the toss, and I want to watch this film."

"Let's have some wine first, shall we?"

Gina smiled and poured Sue a drink.

"I saw Amanda walking out of your gate earlier," Sue said.

"Yeah, I was surprised when I saw her at the door. She wanted to apologise for her reaction when she thought I'd accused her of planting that drug behind my ornament."

"But you did think it was her."

"I still do, actually. I let her in, because what's the point in being hostile, although I didn't speak to her at first. I just think Amanda's under the thumb of *her* next door. I'm being very careful. She wanted to start the massage sessions again."

"You don't trust her, though?"

"No, I don't. I don't trust anyone around here. Except you, of course."

"I appreciate that," Sue said. "So are you going to start up your massage sessions again?"

"I'm still not in the right frame of mind yet. I told her maybe in a couple of weeks."

"When you do, please let me know."

"Yes, of course I will. Are you ready to start the film now?"

"You're sure you want to watch this?"

Gina glanced at Toby above the fireplace. "Yes. Stop worrying about me, Sue. I'm looking forward to it."

She relaxed in her chair, munching crisps and drinking wine as the film started to roll. When the bad guys escaped and John Wick went to his dog, lying motionless, she looked at Toby again with her fists clenched. She took a huge mouthful of wine, her heart thumping against her chest. All she could see was the

TV and Toby. John Wick got to the leader of the gang, and the words "It's just a dog" ripped through her whole body like a machete.

"KILL THE EVIL BASTARD!" she screamed, jumping out of her chair.

Gina felt herself being shaken.

"Gina! Gina!"

She came to, and found herself looking into Sue's angry, shocked eyes. The end credits were rolling.

"What's wrong? Didn't you enjoy it?" she asked. "I thought it was brilliant; I was really into that film."

"Yes!" Sue said. "You really *were* into it, weren't you? Especially the part when you jumped out of your chair and yelled, 'Kill the evil b… bastard.'"

Gina chuckled. "I jumped out of my chair? What are you talking about? I just sat here and watched!"

"You don't remember? I called your name—didn't you hear me?"

"I'm sorry, Sue," Gina said. "I didn't hear you. I would've answered if I did."

"You were tense and angry the whole time, your fists were clenched, you kept looking at Toby. I knew it would affect you."

Gina looked down. Her fists were still clenched. She opened them and saw red marks on her palms.

"Have more wine?" she asked, and Sue held her glass out. "Did I do anything else?" *Were you actually watching the film, or watching me all the time?*

"No. It's just when you jumped out of your chair, you seemed angry like I'd never seen before, like…"

"Like what?" Gina said. "You've seen me angry before, when things happened."

"I don't know if I should say it," Sue said, an odd look on her face.

"Tell me, Sue. Please." Gina's nerves danced inside her stomach.

"It didn't sound like you."

Gina furrowed her brow.

"You were a different person. You sounded different—and before you say anything, yes, I *have* seen you angry, but not like that. Never like that."

Gina shook her head, gave a half-chuckle. "I'm sorry. Sorry if I scared you." She looked at the floor, ashamed. Fear poured over her; if she lost Sue, she'd be completely alone.

"I'm tired," Sue said, getting up to leave. "I need to get to bed."

Gina got out of her chair and grabbed Sue at the door. "Nothing's changed, has it? You're not going to abandon me, are you?"

"No, of course not. I felt it was important to tell you, though. Seeing you like that shocked me more than anything."

"Please don't tell anyone. Especially… you know?" Gina jerked her head towards Tracy's.

"Oh, heavens, no way. I do know what a gossip she can be. And others as well. I do think you should talk about it to Dr… What's his name?"

"Southwell," Gina said. "I will do. Mind you, I'm already on the highest dose of medication, so I don't know what he can do. I'd like to do this again soon, Sue. You can choose the film next time."

CHAPTER THIRTY-SIX

Two weeks went by, and Gina only heard from Sue twice, asking how she was. She kept messaging Sue to suggest another film night, but Sue always said she was busy with her mother. She had no reason to disbelieve her; she knew Sue's mother could partially take care of herself but needed Sue's help constantly. However, niggling doubts entered her mind, especially when she saw Sue talking with Tracy and Eileen, and sometimes Amanda, laughing among themselves outside. Gina wondered if they were talking about her.

Gina wanted to believe Sue, deep down, but wondered if her reluctance to spend another evening together was because of what had happened on their last film night. The fear on Sue's face was stuck in her mind. She kept thinking about what Sue had claimed she'd done, but was still unable to remember any of it.

That afternoon, Gina closed her curtains and watched *John Wick* for the third time since the film night with Sue. She hated the beginning, but the satisfaction she got through the rest of the story captivated her, made her smile. She imagined herself in the lead character's role, doing what he did but to Tracy and Eileen—to anyone who was involved in taking her baby from her.

Gina closed her eyes when the end credits rolled.

Tracy will turn Sue against you.

No, she won't. Sue said she's not going anywhere.

Tracy can be very persuasive.

Sue would never be taken in by her.

The four of them stand outside laughing at your suffering.

No, not Sue. She's my best friend.

Your best friend is laughing with the woman who killed your precious Toby.

"SHUT UP!" Gina yelled.

She felt her phone vibrate, and it lit up. Amanda's name was on the screen.

"Hi, Amanda."

"How are you feeling? I was wondering whether you're feeling ready to start the massage sessions yet? I really need them."

She's tricking you, just like the last time.

"What about Saturday afternoon, around four?"

"That'll be great. Just one thing," Amanda said. Gina took a breath, wondering what was coming. "Can you do it at my house?"

Gina paused. "Yes, no problem. I'll bring my stuff to you."

"You're an angel. Thanks." The line went dead.

Why would Amanda suddenly want the massage at her place?

Because she's tricking you. Again!

What else can they do?

Plant more drugs?

No, they won't do that. The police wouldn't get another warrant after failing the first time.

Take Toby and flush him down the toilet?

She couldn't get in without breaking in.

Doesn't Sue have a key?

She wouldn't do that.

Stupid, naive woman.

***

The following morning, while she sat and drank her coffee, Gina scrolled through the photos of Toby on her phone, for the first time since she lost him. Though sadness crept up inside her, she smiled as she picked out two she really liked. One was of her hugging Toby, their faces together; the other was taken in the park, Toby on his back legs, begging for a chocolate button treat. She looked around the room, thinking she'd love a couple of photo tiles on her wall.

Gina stood up and went to the urn shining on her mantelpiece. Deep in thought, she twisted it a couple of times before taking it to the back garden, where there was a small patio and grass all the way round the fencing. She shook her head, then went back into the house, put the urn in a black plastic bag, put her coat on and headed for the front door.

The leaves crunched under her feet and a sharp, cold breeze blew into her face as she neared the park. She sat on her usual bench, remembering the countless times she'd brought Toby here, the laps they did of the park; Toby chasing after other dogs, only to be stopped by the outstretched lead. There was a Labrador chasing after a frisbee, and she remembered Toby chasing after frisbees thrown by other people for their dogs. She'd always have to pull him back.

The park was quiet that morning—just an old man walking his dog in the distance. Her hands felt icy, and dark clouds began to gather. She spotted the little wooded area that Toby used to explore, and waited till the old man had left the park before wandering over. Under the branches, she took one more look behind her before slowly sprinkling the ashes around the tree.

She hoped she'd done the right thing.

"Goodbye, my baby," she said, looking at the scattered ashes. "I'll never forget you."

CHAPTER THIRTY-SEVEN

On that Saturday morning, Gina took extra medication to keep herself as calm as possible. She felt jittery about going to Amanda's. The last time she'd massaged someone at their own home, it was Annie, who'd died later that night. Gina would never forget what she'd gone through immediately after that.

Though she didn't feel like eating anything, her stomach was rumbling. She made herself some toast with a thin layer of butter and jam.

While eating her breakfast, she browsed through photos of Toby on her phone. How she missed him so much, his cute little face looking back at her.

Amanda's not your friend. She's using you like the last time.

What else can they do to me?

Amanda was involved in killing your poor little dog.

I don't see how or why.

Why does she want you to go to her place?

Maybe she feels more comfortable there?

No. She's trying to trick you. Everyone's against you!

Stop talking rubbish.

Stupid woman.

Gina's phone rang. Sue's number was on the screen.

"Hiya, Sue."

"Fancy another film night tonight?"

"Oh, yes. Definitely."

"How about you come to my place?"

Gina hesitated. "Erm…"

"Don't see a problem, now you haven't got Toby."

Gina didn't respond. She wasn't sure what she felt the most: anger or shock.

Sue sighed in her ear. "Gina, I'm so sorry. I didn't mean it like that. It just came out, and I couldn't stop myself."

After a few seconds, Gina swallowed. "It's alright—I know you didn't mean it like that. I'm at Amanda's this afternoon, then I'll come over."

"Amanda's?" Sue sounded surprised.

"Yeah. She wants me to massage her at her place. She didn't give a reason."

"As long as you're comfortable and not too stressed."

Gina told Sue she'd be round between seven-thirty and eight, then hung up.

Sue doesn't care what happened to Toby, or she wouldn't have said that.

She didn't mean it. She sounded sorry.

She got you out the way so they could carry out their plan.

Gina smacked the side of her head. "SHUT UP!"

She put her candles and a CD into a shoulder bag, put her massage table under her arm and headed out of the door.

∗∗∗

Amanda lived a few doors up, just past the village store. Though it was only a short distance, Gina's arms ached from the weight of the table. Struggling past the white Vauxhall Corsa on the small driveway, she saw Amanda open the front door and unlock the porch door before she had a chance to ring the bell. Amanda was wearing a dark-red silk dressing gown and didn't seem to have anything on underneath.

The living room was spacious, with a big white three-seater sofa facing a large plasma TV on the wall. The room was certainly bright, but Gina thought it could do with more colour.

"I want a full-body massage, if that's alright?" Amanda said. She seemed a bit tipsy, and there was a smell of alcohol on her breath.

Despite her increasing tension, Gina said, "Yep, that'll be fine."

Gina set up her table and placed her candles above Amanda's imitation-log fireplace.

Amanda took off her gown. She was completely naked.

Gina's anxiety shot up.

"Are you alright massaging me like this?" Amanda said.

"Well, my clients normally keep their bottom half covered. I have towels with me, so it's fine."

She lit the candles and put the CD on while Amanda lay on her stomach.

When the massage had begun, Amanda said, "Are you still seeing that detective?"

Gina suddenly stopped rubbing Amanda's shoulders, surprised at the question. "I wasn't actually seeing him. He just came round a few times to either question me or make sure I was alright."

"Mm. It's just I heard you... You know? Did it with him on your sofa."

Gina gave a nervous chuckle as she resumed the massage. "I shouldn't have blurted that out. I knew it would get around."

"Yeah, that may have been a mistake you made."

"What about you?" Gina said. "Anyone special?"

"I haven't been in a relationship for a couple of years now. Nothing serious, anyway—boys or girls."

Gina stopped rubbing her lower back. "Girls?"

"Yeah. I like both. I find women so beautiful, so soft to touch and kiss."

Gina was suddenly very aware of her hands on Amanda's body. "I didn't realise you liked women as well."

"There's nothing shameful in it, Gina."

"No, I agree. You are what you are, and as long as you're happy, that's the main thing."

"Have you ever thought about what it's like to kiss a woman?"

"No. It's never crossed my mind." Gina lifted her hands from Amanda's spine. "And before you think about asking, I'm not going to kiss you."

"I think you might like it. Promise I won't tell anyone."

Gina walked around so they were face to face. "No, Amanda!"

She relaxed her stern look when Amanda nodded and went silent. "Sorry. I didn't mean to snap at you. I've had a rough time since Toby passed away." She resumed the massage.

"I didn't mean to push," Amanda said. "Sue said you told her it was like losing a baby. Personally, I don't see how it can be the same. If you lose a baby, it's like the end of the world, but if you lose your dog or any other pet, you can just get another one. Ouch!"

"I'm sorry," Gina said. "I didn't mean to press so hard."

"That's alright. Someone poisoned him, didn't they? You think it was Tracy?"

She's trying to cause more trouble for you.
No. I just want her to shut up.
She tried to get you to kiss her.
She's had a few drinks. It's fine.

*Now she's trying to get your thoughts on Toby's death.
Tracy put her up to this.*

I'm not going to tell her anything.

*Sue has been talking about you to them. Your so-
called best friend. I told you. They planned this together.*

"Turn onto your back," Gina said. "Try to relax."

"Mm. I'm finding it difficult."

Gina smiled. "That's because you keep talking.
Close your eyes and take deep breaths."

She continued once Amanda had her eyes closed.
The quiet was very welcome; the only sound she heard
was the soft music playing in the background. The
candles continued to burn, giving off a rose scent.
Gina tried to force her mind to stay on what she was
doing, but she kept thinking about what Sue had told
Amanda.

Amanda was calm; her breathing was slow. Gina
rubbed her shoulders and whispered in her ear,
keeping her relaxed. "Amanda. Amanda, wake up.
We're done."

She pulled her, groaning, into a sitting position
and helped her into her dressing gown. Amanda
eventually came to, with Gina still holding her upright.

"How do you feel?"

"Groggy. I could do with a drink."

"Can you trust me to make you a strong coffee?"
Gina giggled. "I might put a drug in there."

"Don't be silly, course I trust you. Search the
cupboards—you'll find mugs and things."

Gina was about to enter the kitchen when there
was a bang on the door.

"Do you mind getting that?" Amanda asked. "I
still feel groggy."

Gina opened the door, and a moment later a large
figure pushed her way past and into the living room.

"You alright, Amanda?" Tracy said.

Gina stood in the living-room doorway, glaring. "She's fine. I was just going to make her a strong coffee."

"You're not making her anything. I'll do it. You just pack up your stuff and get out of here."

Tracy almost pushed her over on her way to the kitchen. Gina just smiled and shook her head.

"I'm sorry," Amanda whispered.

"I'll just get my stuff together and go."

"I'll call you in a couple of days."

Gina opened the front door and stepped outside.

"Why can't you just fucking die like your slut mother and that little mutt?"

As Gina spun around to confront her, Tracy slammed the door in her face.

Gina ground her teeth, and her hand hurt from holding on to the massage table as she trudged through the village towards her house. She was looking forward to going to Sue's, but was also a bit hurt that Sue was talking about her to the others. Losing Toby *was* like losing a real baby. It was a harmless thing to say, and she didn't care that the other neighbours knew. The thing was, what else had Sue been saying to them?

Sue is not your friend. She got you out the way so they could get to Toby.

I don't believe she would ever do that.

You need to confront her about what she told the others.

I don't want to jeopardise our friendship.

You're not her friend.

She's given me support when I needed it.

You can't trust her!

CHAPTER THIRTY-EIGHT

1987

Gina came home late and went straight upstairs.

"Where have you been? You've been gone hours." Lynda followed her. "You answer me, young lady, right now!"

"Nowhere, Mum. I've just been wandering around. I am nearly eighteen, you know."

"You're not eighteen yet. You don't just walk out and disappear for hours like this. I was worried something had happened to you."

"I can take care of myself—quit fussing over me."

"I really don't know what's happened to you lately, Gina. Your attitude is disappointing."

"Attitude! I wanted to help people. I worked hard to become a nurse, passed the exam and everything. But oh no. They refused my application because of my medical history. I can't be a nurse because I'm fucking nuts!"

Heavy footsteps came up the stairs behind her. Before she knew it, Gina had been knocked onto her bed and was holding the side of her face.

"Don't you ever curse like that in this house again, young lady! I don't want to hear from you till the morning."

Gina cried herself to sleep and didn't wake until Lynda came in.

"There's someone to see you downstairs."

She trudged down and froze. Karen's sister stood by the front door. Carol was in a lime-coloured shirt and black trousers; her hair had been cut, and her eyes looked puffy.

"How are you, Gina?" she said.

Gina just shrugged.

"It's been a long time. You've grown into a young woman."

She said nothing and stared at the floor.

"Well, the reason I'm here is to tell you…" Carol paused, wiped her eyes, then continued. "Karen got in an altercation last night and was stabbed in the stomach. She passed away in hospital during the early hours of this morning. She'd… been drinking. The police are investigating, but no witnesses have come forward as yet."

"I'm sorry, Carol," Gina said. Carol gave a slight smile. "I hope the bitch rots in hell."

Carol's face went red.

"Gina!" Lynda yelled as Gina walked back up to her bedroom.

She heard talking downstairs but couldn't hear what was being said and wasn't interested. She just sat on her bed and closed her eyes. The wicked witch was finally gone. Gina smiled and breathed a sigh of relief.

CHAPTER THIRTY-NINE

The next morning, Gina sat eating her toast and sipping her coffee. She'd quite enjoyed her evening with Sue, though she had felt tense when Sue questioned her about her visit to Amanda's. Gina had told her nothing much was talked about, although she did mention how Tracy came and barged her way in. They both laughed. Gina was disappointed she couldn't bring herself to tell Sue about the other stuff Amanda had told her. Normally, she would tell her friend everything, but she was worried Sue would let it out to other people. But she'd enjoyed *Notting Hill*— Sue's choice of film. They both were in stiches at some scenes as the wine went down.

Gina opened her curtains just in time to see Tracy and Sue walking to church together, Tracy chatting away like she normally did. Gina kept watching until they had disappeared into the church grounds. What were they talking about? Knowing Tracy, it would be about Gina. She chuckled when she thought about Tracy showing up at Amanda's, and how quick she had been to stop Gina making the groggy Amanda a drink.

It was going to be a quiet Sunday: her only plans were to do some cleaning, change her bedclothes and spend the rest of the day relaxing with her diamond painting. Her favourite picture of Toby had come through, and she was eager to get it started.

She spent an hour cleaning and got her bedclothes changed, then she sat down and started her diamond painting of Toby. It relaxed her, despite the tinge of sadness when she saw Toby's face and thought about the good times they'd had.

Her peace was soon disturbed as police and ambulance sirens came blasting through the village.

Gina went outside to see what was going on, and the sharp, cold air blew in her face. They'd stopped outside Amanda's house. Though she was wearing her pink woolly jumper, the icy breeze made her shiver. She got her coat and headed towards Amanda's. Her heart was thumping as she drew towards the crowd. Sue, Tracy and Eileen were huddled together on the pavement outside the house. Police tape surrounded Amanda's small driveway, with uniformed officers standing guard.

Gina recognised the unmarked BMW that pulled up even before DS Carter and DI Kene got out. Her mind did overtime as her gaze followed them inside. Had Amanda been assaulted or raped, or even murdered? Gina's mouth had gone dry. Suddenly she winced; when she looked at the back of her hand, she realised she'd scratched it.

Tracy spotted her and said something to Sue and Eileen, who both looked at her. Sue smiled, but the other two gave her a look that said "I want to kill you".

Gina wanted to go back home, close her curtains and hide from the world, but she stayed put, wanting to see what happened and ready for anything that would come her way.

Carter and Kene came out of Amanda's house. Like a shark waiting for its prey, Tracy wasted no time in going straight to them.

They looked in Gina's direction. Kene signalled a uniformed policeman over to him, and they both walked towards Gina, with Tracy lagging behind.

"Miss Wilkinson?" Kene said. "I understand you were with the woman of this house, a Miss Amanda Sullivan, yesterday afternoon?"

"I was, yes," Gina said confidently. "What's happened?"

"What did you do to her?!" Tracy yelled. The uniformed officer had to hold her back.

"I gave her a massage, and that was all—as you well know, Tracy. You came barging in just as I'd finished and practically shoved me out the door." Gina's voice was as calm as she'd ever known.

"How did she seem to you?" Kene asked. "Was she distressed? Did she say anything that might have indicated her mental state?"

"No, nothing like that. I don't even know what's happened."

Kene sighed. "Apparently, Miss Sullivan cut her wrists sometime last night."

Gina went quiet. "Well… She seemed fine when I saw her. I don't understand. I… I can't believe she'd do that." She looked at Tracy, then to Sue, standing on her own.

"Are you sure she didn't say anything that could explain why she'd do such a thing? You have to admit, Miss Wilkinson, it seems odd. Miss Sullivan is the third person you've had contact with who's taken their own life."

Gina went right up to Kene, her arms folded. "She was fine yesterday, from the moment I arrived till the time I left. She was groggy, but that would be expected after a relaxing massage. And I wasn't the last person she had contact with." She looked at Tracy. "*She* was there when I left, and before you get any thoughts of saying I went back later, I was with Sue all evening."

"We know all that, Miss Wilkinson. I'm not accusing you of anything. But as you did have contact with Miss

Sullivan on the day she took her own life, you will remain of interest to this investigation until we find out more information."

"You did something to her, I know you did!" Tracy hissed. "Murderous bitch!"

"You can't pin this one on me. You know she was fine, because you were there when I left."

Tracy ignored her, and Gina followed her gaze towards Amanda's house. Two paramedics were wheeling a stretcher with Amanda wrapped in a black body bag. Tracy started weeping. Eileen came to comfort her, giving Gina a dirty look in the process.

Amanda was put in the ambulance and it drove off slowly—no flashing lights or siren wailing.

"No one's safe in this village as long as she's around!" Tracy yelled. "You need to lock her up and throw away the key!"

"Really?" Gina said. "What reason would I have to kill Amanda? Or make her cut her wrists open?"

"Because you are one fucking crazy bitch, that's why!" Tracy turned to Kene. "She thinks we poisoned her stupid dog."

"Don't you dare call him stupid, you evil cow!" Gina went for Tracy and had grabbed her shoulders before being pulled off by Kene and the PC.

"Go home, Miss Wilkinson," Kene said. "We'll be in contact if we need to ask more questions."

Gina was about to retaliate when Sue came over, took her hand and led her back down towards her house.

"Don't trust her, Sue!" Tracy's voice boomed through the village. "She'll murder us all in the end."

"You need to calm down," Sue said to Gina, once they were inside. "Remember, Tracy's looking for any reason to get you arrested."

"I know. I just couldn't help it. I don't think I've hated anyone so much in my life, apart from Karen. What happened, anyway?"

"Don't know," Sue said. "Tracy got concerned when Amanda didn't show up in church this morning. She's never missed church, and Tracy claims that if she ever did, she would tell her."

"So did she just call the police and they came and checked? I didn't know she had that much influence over them."

"When the service finished, Tracy went straight to Amanda's—she didn't even have her normal coffee after. Apparently, the living-room curtains were open and she saw Amanda slumped over her coffee table."

"Well, they can't pin this one on me. Tracy was with her when I left, and I was with you last night."

"I confirmed that to the police," Sue said. "There's no way you had anything to do with this. I just can't get my head around it. Why would she do that?"

Gina put her hand on Sue's arm and pulled her into a hug. "I don't know, either. On the surface, she seemed fine."

"I've talked with her a few times in the last few weeks," Sue said. "She didn't give any hint something was wrong." Sue started to sob, and Gina held her tighter. Despite her own sadness, no tears would come.

The doorbell rang. To Gina's surprise, Detective Carter was standing there. "Can I come in for a minute?"

"Y… Yes." Gina snapped out of her thoughts and told him to go through to the kitchen. "You can't blame me for this one." She couldn't help going on the defensive right away.

"We know. Mrs Harper told us she saw you leaving Miss Sullivan's and said she seemed fine. She also told us she was with Miss Sullivan for over an hour, and everything seemed normal."

"I'm sorry. I just feel everyone—well, nearly everyone," Gina said, glancing at Sue, "is against me all the time."

"You have one loyal friend here," Carter said. "And I'm not against you. Kene… Well, he has his funny old ways. Doesn't like loose ends, shall we say."

"There are no loose ends in anything. Not to my mind, anyway."

"He still thinks there's loose ends on the Annie Spencer death. He doesn't think it was suicide."

Gina shrugged. "What do you want to ask?"

"I just came to see if you were alright. I saw the commotion you had with Mrs Harper."

"I didn't mean to yell like that in front of everyone. Emotions were running high and I overreacted. She said I did something to Amanda before she turned up, then she called my Toby stupid. I just lashed out."

"We all do that from time to time. Kene's going to come and see you to get a statement on events yesterday."

"Can't you do that?" Gina said, following him to the door.

"I did offer, but he said he'd rather do it."

Gina sighed and shook her head.

After Carter left, she went back to the kitchen. Sue was at the sink, wiping the black marks under her eyes.

"How are you feeling?" Gina asked.

"I feel better," Sue said. "Sometimes a good cry is what you need at a time like this."

"Kene's coming to see me about a statement. I don't want that man in my house."

"I'll stay with you."

"Ah, thanks. I'll feel better with you here."

"I don't understand why Carter couldn't get a statement from you. Do you think the inspector knows?"

"That I had sex with Carter? Yes—I blurted it out, didn't I?"

"Not a smart move on your part, Gina."

"Oh well. He was off duty, and even police officers are supposed to be free."

The doorbell rang again.

"Right, here goes," Gina said.

She opened the door and put on a fake smile. Kene was standing there, not looking impressed at all.

"We need a statement regarding yesterday's events, Miss Wilkinson." He didn't move when she opened the door to let him in. "We need you to make it at the station."

Gina relaxed her fake smile. "No way. You're not tricking me into going in that place."

"It's just a statement, then you can come straight home."

"I'll go with you, Gina," Sue said.

Gina sighed. "When? Now?"

"No. Actually, I'm about to take Mrs Harper to the station for her statement, so I think it's probably wise you *don't* come now. Tomorrow will do, or the next day. But don't leave it too long."

CHAPTER FORTY

The next day, Gina and Sue arrived at the police station. Though Gina had taken extra medication, she wanted to walk out as soon as she went in; the place had the same sterile aroma as a hospital. Her hands grew clammy while she waited at the desk.

After she'd announced herself to the sergeant, they escorted her into a room very similar to the one she'd been interrogated in just after Annie was found on her lawn. Gina sat on the hard wooden chair while Sue remained standing. They were in there for a good fifteen minutes, which seemed like over an hour to Gina, not knowing what to say to each other. Suddenly the door opened and a uniformed policeman came in. He was taller than Gina, and she saw ginger hair under his police cap. He announced himself as PC Benson and asked Gina to run through what had happened yesterday while she was with Amanda, to the exact detail.

"I didn't sense anything wrong—from the time I arrived, through the massage itself, right to when I left."

"What did you talk about?" Benson said.

There was a pause. "She did blurt out something personal. I don't know why she told me this, but she did."

He looked at her, urging Gina to continue.

"Amanda told me she was bisexual. She hadn't revealed that information before." Gina glanced at Sue and saw the surprise on her face. "I was surprised at the time."

"She didn't talk about any failed relationship or anything?"

"Nope. She didn't talk about anything that I thought would cause her distress or would make me think she'd take her own life. Although I also found out she used to take drugs years ago. Don't know if she was back on them, but I didn't see any strange signs that made me think she might be." Gina waited for him to finish writing.

"Anything else at all?"

"No. As I got her relaxed, she went quiet… Then just as I'd finished, Tracy Harper came in and I left."

"If you have no more to add, can you read and sign that, please?"

Gina quickly read through the statement, then signed the paper at the bottom.

She was about to walk out of the station with Sue when a familiar voice called out to her. She cringed inside as the deep Scottish accent drowned her ears. Inspector Kene was standing behind her, his stomach bulging out over his trousers. He quickly looked over the statement she'd signed, then thrust it back at PC Benson.

"I hope you haven't left anything out, Miss Wilkinson. Very important you tell us everything."

Gina rolled her eyes. She'd heard all this before.

"We're looking into Miss Sullivan's death closely. The post-mortem should tell us whether she took anything or was given something unknowingly."

Gina folded her arms and got as close as she could get to Kene. "If Amanda did take something that made her do this, you'll find it impossible to *prove* I forced her to take whatever you think it was. You can't help yourself, can you? Trying to accuse me of causing another suicide."

"Just like you're convinced Mrs Harper killed your dog by poison. Am I right, Miss Wilkinson?"

Adrenaline rose in her body. "She *did* poison Toby. Either that or she got someone else to do it. Who else?" She didn't take her eyes off him.

He chuckled. "Come on, Miss Wilkinson, you probably poisoned the little devil yourself, then shifted the blame to your neighbour." Kene carried on laughing.

"Bastard!" She slapped his face.

Before she could say another syllable, Gina was pushed against the wall. She struggled, but her hands were forced behind her and cuffed. She got turned around to face Sue, who had her hand over her mouth.

Kene glared at her, still holding his hand to the side of his face. "I'm sure you know assaulting a police officer is a serious offence?"

Gina breathed heavily; her eyes burned with tears.

"You could do prison time for that."

She didn't say anything.

"However. Too much paperwork and too much hassle, so I'm going to let this pass with a warning. You'll slip up, Miss Wilkinson, and I'll get you on a more serious charge." Kene gave a nod to the policewoman holding her, and the cuffs were taken off. "Get out of my sight!"

Sue grabbed Gina's arm and pulled her out of the station. "What on earth were you thinking?"

Gina didn't answer, and dashed off to the bus stop.

They sat at the back of the bus, where it was empty.

"You slapped the face of a police officer. And not just any officer—he's a top senior. And you called him a b… the B word."

Gina stared out of the window in silence. As Sue started to speak again, she held up her hand. "I don't want to talk about it."

When they both got to Gina's gate, she turned to Sue. "You don't hate me, do you?"

"Course not. I'm not going to suddenly hate you. You need to sort yourself out, though. That could've been a lot more serious."

Gina nodded. "I'd rather be alone, if you don't mind. I'll call you soon."

She went inside and got herself a gin and tonic, unable to stop shaking. Realising how lucky she'd been not to be charged, she grabbed her phone and called Dr Southwell's secretary for an appointment as soon as she could get one. There wasn't any availability till the following week.

***

Gina didn't leave the house for the rest of the week. She spoke twice to Sue on the phone, but there was no other contact. She kept herself busy doing her household chores and her diamond painting and crochet; she even put together a jigsaw puzzle of a cottage and garden that had been gathering dust upstairs.

Late in the afternoon of the day before she was due to see Dr Southwell, DS Carter paid her a visit. She was uncomfortable about having contact with anybody but didn't want to appear rude, so let him in. He was on duty, judging by the suit he was wearing.

"I came to let you know Miss Sullivan's death was ruled a suicide. I would've let you know sooner, but you know how it is."

Gina nodded. "I didn't expect anything else, really."

"I heard what happened at the station when you made your statement. I don't know what made you do that, but you were—"

"Very lucky. Yes, I know. I don't have to keep hearing it. He accused me of poisoning my Toby. How dare he say that?"

There was an awkward silence.

"Are you going to Miss Sullivan's funeral next week?" Carter said, like it was the only thing he could think of saying.

"Probably not, no. Personal reasons."

Carter nodded, then walked to the door. Gina was right behind him.

Suddenly he turned and drew his mouth towards hers, but she turned away and pushed him slightly.

"Please don't," she said sadly.

She held her hand in front of his face, then shut the door as soon as he left.

CHAPTER FORTY-ONE

The next day, Gina was up early. She'd had a restless night, so downed two coffees before getting ready to see Dr Southwell. She was always slightly anxious before she saw him. Although he was there to help her, he also had the power to have her sectioned if he felt it appropriate.

She arrived at the clinic a few minutes early and was pleased to see the waiting room empty.

"Hello, Gina love. How are you?" the receptionist, a woman with small round glasses, said. She always smiled when she saw Gina. "Take a seat. Dr Southwell won't be a moment."

Gina sat down. She tried to control her breathing but shivered slightly.

Within a couple of minutes, she was sitting opposite Dr Southwell in his room. There was the normal silence, each waiting for the other to say something.

"Why did you ask to see me, Gina?" he asked. "What's on your mind?"

It's a wonder my mind hasn't exploded out of my head.

"Well, some things have been happening, apparently," she said.

Southwell stayed silent.

"You know I lost my dog, Toby?"

"Yes, you said the last time you saw me. How have you been coping?"

Gina hesitated, then began to tell him about the night she'd watched *John Wick* with Sue, when she'd apparently jumped out of her chair, screaming at the TV screen. That vision of Sue's shocked face was still in her head. Southwell didn't respond, but she knew he was listening.

"The thing is," she said, "when the film was over and Sue told me what I did, I had no recollection of it, of doing any of it. I thought she might have been joking, but the look on her face told me she wasn't."

"My wife is a Keanu Reeves fan," Southwell said. "She's watched every film he's made. Sometimes when I'm not so busy, I watch them with her. I've actually seen that film. His character gets revenge on some thugs who attack him at his home and kill his dog."

Gina nodded, surprised at his openness; she'd thought doctors of any profession wouldn't say anything to patients about their private lives. It relaxed her more, knowing he felt comfortable enough around her to say what his wife liked, even though it was just her favourite actor.

"Maybe you just got overexcited," he said. "Maybe you saw it as yourself, wanting to get revenge for what happened to your dog."

"I don't think I'm capable of killing anyone."

"I didn't mean it like that."

"Then there's Amanda," Gina said.

"Amanda?"

"One of my neighbours. She, um, killed herself." Gina swallowed. She tried to study Southwell, but his expression didn't change. "She was found Sunday morning. She'd cut her wrists." She took a breath. "The thing is, on the Saturday afternoon, I gave her a massage."

"How did she seem?"

"Fine. I didn't notice anything different about her— she seemed her normal self."

"Did you get accused of being involved, like the others?"

"I got questioned, but they couldn't accuse me this time because I had an alibi. My neighbour Tracy came to check on Amanda just after the massage, to see if I'd done anything to her. She practically shoved me out the door as soon as she got there."

"Oh—it wasn't done at your home, then?"

"No. Amanda requested to be massaged at her place. She never said why."

"There you go, then. You can't be accused of this one."

"She tried—Tracy, that is. She accused me of going back later that night. But I was with Sue all evening."

"So, you have nothing to worry about. You've done nothing wrong."

"I had to make a statement at the police station. That's the other thing I wanted to talk about."

That's it, you'll be back in that place; he'll section you straight away.

He won't put me back there.

You'll never get out.

"It's all right, Gina. Tell me. Remember, I'm here to help you."

"I went to the police station, to make a statement. Sue came with me for support." She breathed deeply. "After I'd finished, I bumped into Inspector Kene on my way out. He read through the statement I made. Then he went on about how I'd accused Tracy of killing Toby. I've told you how much he meant to me." Southwell nodded. "Kene laughed, he laughed in my face, and said I probably poisoned Toby myself to place the blame on her." Silence fell in the room. "I called him a bas—well, the B word—then slapped his face."

"So you assaulted a police officer? A senior police officer?"

Gina nodded, her eyes starting to burn.

"Are you being charged?"

She shook her head. "They pushed me against the wall and handcuffed me, but he said something about paperwork and too much hassle."

"You were very lucky, then."

Tears rolled down her cheeks. "I just zoned out. I didn't realise I did it. It's like something took over—I couldn't stop myself."

That's it. Go and pack your stuff. Say goodbye to your nice little house.

"SHUT UP!" Gina leant forward with her head in her hands.

"Excuse me?" Southwell said.

"I want the voice in my head to shut up."

"What's the voice saying?"

"That you're going to put me away, and I'll never get out this time."

"Well, ignore the voice. I'm not going to put you anywhere." Dr Southwell's voice was so gentle, she wanted to sink into his arms right then. She didn't feel rushed; he seemed to give her all the time she needed. When she had these sessions with him, she often thought how lucky his wife was to have a husband like him.

"I want him back. I miss my baby so much. I want him back!"

He handed her another tissue, and she just sobbed.

"Sometimes I'm okay, but other times I'm hurting really bad. I'm sorry," she said, dabbing her eyes over and over.

Southwell gave a sympathetic smile. "Why are you saying sorry? You should let it out from time to time. The worst thing you can do is hold it all in, have it bottled up inside you. I understand losing Toby is like you've lost your own child."

Gina nodded vigorously. She wanted to jump up and just throw her arms around him. But she stayed in her seat. She wasn't going to make the mistake of getting too close to her psychologist again—not after what had happened with Dr Griffin.

She'd started having sessions with Joe about ten years ago, and when she was at her low points, he would offer her a hug. It was just hugging for a while; then he kissed her, and the kisses became more passionate as time went on. He moved Gina's care on to another psychologist so they could have a relationship. She'd lived with Joe for three years, moved into his house, and it was wonderful at first; he was kind, spoke in a gentle voice and took care of her. But then things changed. He became suddenly aggressive and distant—and one day, he asked her to leave, out of the blue. Gina had rented a flat nearby until she moved to the village. The only person she'd ever talked to about her relationship with Joe was Sue.

"You're not only hurting, but you're angry," Southwell said. "Sometimes you may not feel angry, but it's there, bubbling away inside you."

Gina nodded. "Sometimes I feel fine, but there are times when I just want to scream my head off for no reason. My friend Sue comforts me, but then I see her talking to Tracy. She knows the situation between us, but every time I see them together, I can't help but think they're talking about me. What does Sue really think of me? What does she say behind my back?" She shook her head vigorously. "They stand outside. I saw them a few times out the window—the four of them, Tracy, Eileen, Amanda and Sue, all huddled together, laughing. Sometimes Tracy glances at my window, as if she knows I'm looking. I stand at a distance so they can't see me through the net curtain…" Gina paused, waiting, but Southwell kept silent. "She's trying to take Sue away from me. My best friend. The bitch took my beloved dog, now she's taking my best friend!" Gina's voice was low; she ground her teeth. Southwell didn't flinch. He just watched. "I had nothing to do with what happened with Karen and her dad."

She jumped out of her chair.

Southwell remained seated, still observing.

"Everyone hates me! Karen ruined my childhood, instead of leaving me alone. Now that fat bitch is trying to make my life hell!" Gina screamed.

Southwell finally stood up, grabbed her by the arms and sat her down.

"It's alright." Although Gina was shaking and sobbing, his voice was as calm as an ocean on a hot sunny day. "What you have is EUPD—emotionally unstable personality disorder." She just looked at him. "Mood changes, intense anger, paranoia, feeling rejected. Do you drink?" She nodded. "This condition is almost certainly caused by what you went through as a child."

"I do stuff without realising. Is that part of it?"

"Yes, definitely. Bad things have happened to you— it seems one bad thing after the other. You're not a bad person. You just have issues, mainly due to what's happened to you."

"Did I do something, then—to Annie and Amanda?"

"No, I'm sure you didn't. There's no evidence that you were involved in anything."

"I had contact with them just before they died."

"Doesn't mean you were involved in their deaths. Some people just end it. I need to ask, Gina—have *you* thought about suicide since I saw you last?"

"No. Honestly, I haven't. I did before I saw you, but not now." She held her breath as he studied her face.

He gave a smile. "What I want you to do is go and have a hot bath—lots of bubbles—and try to relax. I'll write to your GP to see if you can have some stronger antidepressants. Try to ignore any voices inside your head. Do what relaxes you and what you enjoy doing. Keep yourself occupied. I'll see you again in a month or so."

CHAPTER FORTY-TWO

Over the next few weeks, Gina took hot, bubbly baths instead of showers. She did her diamond painting and colour by numbers—even a jigsaw—and when she felt frustrated, she'd close her eyes and take deep breaths. The only time she saw Tracy was when they passed each other in the street on the day of Amanda's funeral. Gina was the only village resident who didn't attend; she went to the village store instead, and passed Tracy on her way home. They blanked each other, which suited Gina. She wished it would always be like that instead of the snide, bitchy comments Tracy normally came out with.

In fact, the village had gone quiet again. Tracy hadn't been standing in her front garden talking like she used to. Gina heard that Amanda's suicide had affected her in quite a big way—though she did wonder if Tracy was also upset that she couldn't blame Gina this time.

There had been no contact from the police since the incident with Kene, though she kept wondering if he would change his mind and charge her with the assault.

Gina talked with Sue a few times on the phone—but when she asked if they could meet up for a chat, Sue told her she was looking after her mother and couldn't leave her at the moment. Gina told her about the appointment with Dr Southwell, and noticed the concern in Sue's voice when she talked about how the loss of Toby was maybe causing her to have this sudden anger issue.

She often looked at pictures of Toby. She couldn't help it; she missed him like crazy. The voices in her head kept telling her to take revenge for his death, but she tried to ignore them. There was nothing she would like more, but she had no proof—though she was almost certain who was involved. She was still determined to find out the truth. She couldn't rest fully without knowing for sure what had happened or who exactly had poisoned him. Did Tracy do it herself? Or did she get someone else to put those biscuits through the letterbox, not wanting to be seen?

***

On a crisp, cold morning three weeks after her appointment, Gina left the house and went to the park. She wandered into the small wooded area where she'd sprinkled Toby's ashes. It was the first time she'd been to the park since then. She stood there and imagined Toby in an open field, running wild and free.

On her way back, she was nearing Eileen's house when George came out with a rubbish bag. He was limping slightly, but other than that he looked to be in good health. He wore octagonal glasses and still had a full head of hair.

"Hello, George!"

He jumped a little.

"How are you? I haven't seen you around in some time. You're looking fit and well, I must say."

"Not looking so bad yourself, Gina," he said. At seventy-five, George was the oldest resident in the village. His voice sounded strong; Gina knew he never smoked or drank. "I'd best go in. Eileen will be back soon. She'll be getting herself ready for tonight."

"Tonight?"

"Yeah. She's going out with Tracy and Sue. Tracy said they should spend time together after what happened with Amanda." George shook his head. "Shocking!"

"It certainly was. I'm surprised Sue's going—I understood she's looking after her mother."

"They're picking her up from her mother's—it's only around the corner. That's what Eileen told me, anyway."

Gina headed home, glancing at Sue's house as she passed.

Back inside her own four walls, she stood at the sink, shaking her head. She remembered the conversation she'd had with Sue.

"Can we meet up somewhere?" Gina had asked.

"It's very difficult to leave Mum right now. She's suffering with her leg. You know how arthritis gets? Some good days and some bad ones. I'll probably have to end up moving in with her not long from now."

Gina sat in her living room and gathered her thoughts. Why would Sue say that to her, then go out with Tracy and Eileen?

She's against you. That's why.

No way. She's been so nice and supportive.

It's all an act. Her mind's been poisoned. She's with her now. She got you out of the house, allowing them to kill Toby.

Later that evening, Gina looked through her photos of Toby once more. She stared at the photo of both of them, taken by Sue when they were in the park. She smiled at his cute little face and wiped away a tear that was running down her cheek. Her hands were red from where she'd clenched her fists so tight.

She got up, put on her dark-blue coat, pulled the hood over her head and headed out of the door. It was dark, and the icy wind stung her face as she stepped outside. She looked up and down, making sure Tracy's Mini was nowhere in the village; then she walked to Eileen's house and knocked on the door.

It opened a crack, George's eyes peering through. "What do you want?" he asked hesitantly.

"I need to talk to you."

"I can't talk to you!" George tried to shut the door, but she put her foot in the gap to block it. "Will you please go away, Gina! I've got things to do."

She didn't move her foot. The pleasant smile that she'd worn when she spoke to him earlier was replaced with a scornful look. "You're going to talk to me, George. I'll be gone before they get back."

He let Gina through the passage into the living room.

This was the first time Gina had been in Eileen's house, and she knew Eileen would be furious if she found out. The living room was bigger than hers, with an open fireplace. The walls were lime green, and there was a big beige leather sofa and a matching recliner chair. French doors opened to a large conservatory leading to the back garden. It looked very clean and tidy.

George went and sat down. "What do you want, Gina?" he asked again.

"I think you know what happened to Toby."

He leapt out of his chair. "What makes you think I know?"

"Toby was poisoned, Tracy hates my guts, Eileen is her best friend. You and Eileen are retired chemists. I know they did this, George. And you know it too, don't you?"

George looked at the floor, unable to meet her eyes.

Gina crouched down, putting her hand on his arm. "Toby was my life, George. His death has left a massive empty space inside me." George finally looked up at her, in time to see the tear running down her cheek. "I miss him so much—the walks we took; he followed me around the house, cuddled up to me at night. It was like having my own baby. And he was my aid when I had to go out on my own. Although, in a lot of people's words, it's only a dog, the loss is just as heartbreaking."

"I used to watch you go past our window with him," George said. "He was the cutest little fellow I'd ever seen." He smiled for the first time since Gina had arrived, and seemed more relaxed.

"He was a wonderful little dog," Gina said. "He took a bit of time getting used to me, but once he did, he wouldn't leave me alone. And I wouldn't have had it any other way."

"I don't understand why you're disliked around here. I think you're really nice."

"Thank you, George. I *am* really nice, but I'm also very heartbroken. So what happened?"

Shaking his head, he looked away from her again. "I can't. I'll get into so much trouble. It would be more than my life's worth."

"No one will ever find out we had this conversation."

"What are you going to do?"

"Nothing I can do, really. I just want to know. It's eating away at me."

"I overheard Eileen and Tracy talking about it," George said. "Eileen never spoke to me directly about it—I just overheard their conversation."

Gina started rubbing his shoulders. "Just relax, George, and tell me what you heard."

"Tracy told Eileen she wanted you to suffer like her mum suffered. They talked about the one thing you loved and cherished in this world. Your dog, Toby."

CHAPTER
FORTY-THREE

When her alarm went off, Gina just lay there, wondering if there was any point in getting up. What reason did she have to face the day?

Why had Sue lied to her? Was she really her friend, or just using her in some way?

Her chest tightened as a sharp pain shot through her. Gina ducked under her covers and closed her eyes.

She tore her eyes open; her phone was ringing on the bedside table. She scrambled for it and saw Sue's name. For a moment, she thought about letting it ring out. However, after thirty seconds, she answered.

"Gina! Gina, have you heard?" Sue spoke fast. Gina could barely understand.

"Sue, slow down. What's wrong? Is it your mother?"

"No. Tracy just called me." Gina rolled her eyes. "Something's happened at Eileen's. Didn't you hear any sirens or anything?"

"Sirens? No, I didn't."

Gina scrambled out of bed and went to her spare room.

Two ambulances and police cars were outside Eileen's big house. Tracy was being consoled by a policewoman, and DS Carter and DI Kene were standing on the driveway.

She put some clothes on and wandered up to see what had happened. She kept her distance, but suddenly she heard someone scream, "What have you *done*, BITCH?!"

Tracy's large figure was marching towards her. Gina froze on the spot. She thought Tracy was going to just scream in her face, and she was prepared for that—Tracy couldn't do much else in front of police officers—but without warning, Tracy pushed her hard to the ground, then got on top of her.

Pain stabbed Gina's lip. She wiped it and saw blood on her hand, then another sharp pain cracked at the back of her head as it hit the pavement.

In her blurred vision, she saw two figures pull Tracy off her; then a policewoman helped Gina up, took her to Eileen's garden wall and sat her down. The pain in her head was throbbing. Her vision returned just in time to see Tracy sitting in the back of a police car.

Carter came over and asked if she was alright. "Do you want to press charges for assault?"

Gina shook her head.

Then Kene approached. "Sorry about what happened there, Miss Wilkinson. Emotions are running high after what's happened. Mrs Harper is very distressed right now. I can't stop you taking it further, but with no harm done, I'd ask you to consider whether it's really necessary."

Gina gave him a look, then smiled. "I'm not pressing charges. Can't deal with the hassle."

Kene walked off without saying anything else.

Gina's attention turned back to Tracy in the back of the police car. Her mascara had run and she looked a mess.

"I want to go home," Gina said.

"Hold on, I'll walk you home," Carter offered. "You shouldn't go on your own. Just wait there for a minute." He went over to Kene, the two had a lengthy discussion, and after about five minutes, he came back.

"You should have medical attention," he said.

"I'm fine. I feel better now," she lied.

"Kene wants me around here. My colleague here will walk you home, and I'll come and see you shortly."

Gina walked home with the young policewoman, then went in and sat in her chair once she'd told the officer there was no need to stay—she was fine.

"Why didn't I stay in bed?" she said out loud to no one.

There was a knock at the door. Gina got up and had to stand still as pain throbbed in her head. She staggered to the door and was pleased to see Carter standing there on his own; she wasn't sure she could have taken Kene's Scottish voice booming questions at her right then.

"How are you feeling?" Carter said.

"I'm alright. Do you want anything?"

"No, I'm fine, thanks."

They went to the living room. She sat in her normal chair, but seeing Carter sitting on her sofa—the sofa they'd made love on—made her body tingle.

"What on earth happened?" she asked.

"Tracy Harper was frantic. She said she went out with Eileen Levin and Sue Houldsworth two nights ago."

Gina rolled her eyes.

"Mrs Harper planned to meet Mrs Levin yesterday evening at the village pub. She thought Mrs Levin was unwell when she didn't show up. But when she tried to call this morning and didn't get an answer, she went to her house—apparently, she has a key. She went to check to see if Mrs Levin was alright, and found her on the floor in a bloody mess. It looks like she was attacked with an axe. It was lying beside her."

Gina slowly looked away from him. There was a lump stuck in her throat, and she felt she couldn't speak if she'd wanted to.

"She ran out of the house, screaming. Neighbours came out to calm her down, and that's when we got the call."

"And she thinks *I* did it?"

"She's in an emotional state, not thinking straight."

"Do you have any idea who might have done it?" Gina said.

"It's a bit early, but the main suspect is her husband, George."

Gina's mouth fell open. "George? No! Why on earth would he do that?"

"We won't know until we've gathered all the evidence. The axe was driven into Mrs Levin's forehead not just once, but a few times—that's what it looked like to me. There was blood everywhere. Carpet, sofa, the walls had blood spatter. It looked like something from a horror film. The Levins must have had an argument and he flew into a rage."

"He's seventy-five years old," Gina said. "I didn't realise he could be that strong."

"You'd be surprised. If they look after themselves through the years, even eighty-plus-year-olds can be strong."

"Has George been arrested?" Gina said.

Carter sighed. "No. We can't arrest him or even question him."

"Why not?"

There was a pause. "Because he's dead. We found him hanging from his bedpost."

"I… I don't know what to say. It's just…"

"Shocking?" Carter said.

She nodded. "I talked with him a couple of days ago, and he seemed alright—a little nervous, maybe, but that was because he didn't want to be seen talking to me. I thought Eileen had control of George, not the other way around."

"You'd be surprised what you think you know and what actually happens behind closed doors." Carter got up and headed for the door. "Under the circumstances, I think you made a wise decision not to press charges against Mrs Harper."

"I don't want any more hassle. I made that decision for me, not her."

Carter smiled. She grabbed his arm as he was about to leave, and pulled him towards her. They kissed gently.

"I'll let you know more details when I find out."

Gina took her meds, then called Sue and told her what Carter had said. She also mentioned Tracy's attack.

"Why does everyone think I'm guilty when something happens?" she said.

"I don't know." Sue's voice was shaky. "I can't understand—George would never attack anyone. Something's not right here. I'm totally lost as to what's going on in the village right now."

"I don't know either," Gina said. "Just need to wait for further news."

"I'm coming home tomorrow anyway."

"You want to come over so we can talk?"

"I will do, Gina, but I want to see how Tracy's doing. The poor thing must be in a right state after what she found. Imagine seeing your best friend like that… She needs all the love and support she can get. It's a pity you both have such hatred towards each other. I think in situations like this and with what's gone on in this village lately, we all need to support each other. I'll see you soon, Gina."

CHAPTER FORTY-FOUR

Just over a week had gone by since Eileen and George were found dead in their home. Gina didn't leave the house, and she had hardly any contact with Sue—but she did see Sue and Tracy going in and out of each other's houses. She wanted to try to give Sue space and let her support Tracy. She'd meant to call Sue yesterday to see how she was and ask her to come over, but again put it off.

Gina was starting to wonder if she had lost her best friend. Her mind kept going back to the time Sue went out with Tracy and Eileen, when she'd told Gina she couldn't leave her mother. Why did people always let her down?

I kept telling you.

She could've popped over to see me.

She's her *best friend now, not yours.*

They're always together. Did Sue show this much love and support when I lost Toby?

Toby's a dog. He didn't matter to Sue.

Dogs are more loyal than people.

A knock at the door made Gina jump. She looked out of the window and saw Detective Carter. She opened the door and followed him to the living room.

"How are you?" he said.

Gina shrugged. "As well as I can be, I suppose. Do you want anything?"

"No, I'm on duty, thanks. I just came by to let you know about the inquests for Mr and Mrs Levin."

Gina gave a smile. "I'm flattered. You didn't have to do that. I wasn't close to either of them—quite the opposite, as you know."

"Mr Levin committed the act; there's no doubt about that. The evidence is clear. I don't know what made him go into such a rage all of a sudden, but he did make quite a mess."

"I talked to him a couple of days before. He was a sweet old man. Apart from the slight limp he had, he seemed quite fit and healthy."

"What's shocking, though, is why he did it in the first place," Carter said. "Couples have their problems, no doubt about that, but it takes a certain mindset and rage to swing an axe at someone's head."

"I'm shocked about it as well," Gina said. "Me and Eileen never liked each other—she was like her next door—but I can't possibly think what she did or said to make George do something like that. Perhaps his mind just went funny, I don't know. Then he hanged himself."

Carter nodded. "It can happen, particularly when you get older. We thought maybe he didn't want to live any more, wanted to take his wife with him. Killed her, then himself."

Gina shook her head. "While everything might seem rosy on the outside, you never know what's going on behind closed doors."

"The funeral's tomorrow," Carter said.

"I didn't know."

"No one told you?"

Gina shook her head. "It was obvious I wouldn't be going."

"I thought Sue would've told you?"

She looked away from him. "I haven't seen her much lately, since Eileen and George were found. She'd been looking after her mum, and since she got back, she's been with…" She swallowed.

Carter nodded. He put his arms around Gina and held her gently; she didn't resist. He was warm, and she felt secure in his arms.

"Mrs Harper was very affected when she found Mrs Levin. Maybe your friend is just giving her extra support."

"I understand that," she said. "It's just… I've called Sue and texted her to come over for a coffee and a chat. She always says she can't right now but promises she will sometime. Surely she has time to talk to me?"

"I understand what you mean," Carter said. "You feel neglected, don't you?"

Gina nodded, and he held her tighter. "She always had time for me. I think I've lost her to… you know?"

"No, you haven't. She's just a friendly neighbour taking care of someone who's in an emotional state right now."

"You don't understand, Jack. That woman hates me so much, she's trying to punish me by driving a wedge between me and Sue. She's probably poisoned Sue's mind with so much crap about me. I know she blamed me for this, like the rest."

Carter didn't say anything. He took her by surprise, cupped her face and locked their lips together.

"I should go," he said, when he pulled away. He went to leave, but Gina pulled him back. "I'm on duty," he said, laughing.

She didn't seem to hear. She pulled off his jacket, unbuttoned his shirt. He tried to stop her, but she slapped his hand away and pulled him onto the sofa.

Afterwards, they sat together, panting and laughing.

"I really must go," he said.

"If anyone asks why you were in here so long, just tell them I was in a state and you were trying to calm me down."

Carter quickly got dressed and left. As Gina went to shut the door behind him, she saw Sue walking up towards Tracy's front door. Their eyes met, and Gina forced a smile before closing the door.

She felt sick to her stomach every time she saw them together, and she couldn't understand why her best friend would no longer have much contact with her. She had thought their friendship was strong.

Whenever Tracy said anything cruel to Gina, Sue would tell her to ignore it. *Don't let her get into your head or under your skin.* But Sue had done exactly what she'd told Gina not to do: she'd let Tracy get inside her head. And now suddenly she believed everything Tracy said. Gina knew Tracy talked about her constantly, and now she had Sue in her clutches.

Gina took a heavy dose of sleeping pills, despite having been told by her doctor that it could be dangerous. However, they did the trick. She slept through the night, and when her alarm went off at seven, she turned it off, unable to think of a reason to get up. She still felt drowsy, so she hid herself under the covers and went back to sleep. When she finally woke up from what she would describe as a beautiful sleep, she slowly got herself out of bed and trudged downstairs, passing the mirror in the hall. Her hair was a mess and her eyes were droopy.

She made a coffee and sat down in her chair, wondering what another day would bring. Nothing. Just another day. The sun shone bright through her curtains, and it was only then she realised she hadn't looked at the time. When she fired up her phone, she couldn't believe it was gone one in the afternoon.

Staring at the sofa, she thought about Carter and couldn't help grinning. Then her stomach rumbled, so she went to the kitchen. She hadn't eaten much in the last couple of days, nor had she left the house. There wasn't much left in her cupboards; she'd have to pay a visit to the village store. She sighed and tutted, but she went upstairs and put on a woolly top and some leggings.

On her way to the store, Gina saw two coffins being carried into the village church. Sue was standing alongside them, hugging Tracy, who looked to be sobbing.

Gina walked on, not wanting to be seen, and hurried back home as soon as she was done.

CHAPTER FORTY-FIVE

Later that evening, Gina texted Sue again, asking if she'd like to come for a chat. She really missed her chats with Sue, and Sue's company, but again she was left disappointed when Sue texted back an hour later that she couldn't make it. Gina knew the timing hadn't been right to ask—Sue had been with Tracy at the Levins' funeral—but she couldn't help but think she had lost her friend. What had Tracy told Sue about her? What lies had she been spilling?

Her chest started to hurt. She took Toby's photo off the mantelpiece and stared at it.

"I wish you were here, my gorgeous baby," she said. "You would've stayed loyal to me forever." She kissed him, then put the photo back.

Gina took another dose of sleeping pills that night, and again slept right through. Her alarm woke her, but she turned it off and went back to sleep.

A hammering sound woke her. She rubbed her eyes, then looked at her phone; half-one in the afternoon. The hammering kept going, and she realised someone was knocking at her door. She trudged downstairs, squinting in the bright sunlight, the drowsiness still inside her. It took a few seconds for her to see Sue standing at her door.

The atmosphere was instantly tense, but Gina allowed her in.

"I sorry I haven't been in contact much," Sue said. "It's just been crazy around here with what's happened. First Amanda, then George and Eileen."

"I know," Gina said. "I missed your company, that's all. It just doesn't seem like it was before."

"Gina, people are dead! Our neighbours are dead."

Gina folded her arms and looked away. "I know that."

"You hide yourself from the outside world so much. I mean, look at you. It's well into the afternoon, and you look like you just got out of bed."

"That's because I have." Gina turned away from Sue and looked out of the window. "I wake up in the morning when my alarm goes off, and I lie there looking for a reason to get up and start the day, and I can't think of one."

"You feel like I've neglected you, I understand that, but all this has affected me, and it's affected Tracy even worse. I just felt she needed support. I know the two of you don't get along, but Tracy seeing that scene in her best friend's house—you can't imagine what that's like. Blood everywhere, Eileen's head practically split open. No wonder the poor love was traumatised by it all."

"She does have Colin for support. You know—her husband?"

"They haven't been getting along too well lately. They always go hot and cold. In fact, Tracy's convinced Colin doesn't love her any more."

"How was the funeral?" Gina said, trying to break the tension.

"It was nice, but Tracy didn't cope with it too well. George and Eileen were buried next to each other in the cemetery."

Gina nodded but didn't really hear. "I thought I'd lost my best friend," she said. "I thought she'd succeeded in turning you against me."

Sue tutted. "Come here, you daft thing." She pulled Gina into a hug. "I'll always be your friend. How about

I come round tomorrow afternoon, and you can give me a wonderful massage?"

Gina chuckled. "Any time. You could stay for the evening. I could do us some food and we can watch a film?"

Sue looked awkward. "Erm... Can we make that another time?"

"Yeah, sure." Gina tried to sound upbeat and forced a smile.

"Next week sometime? I've just got... you know?"

"I'm not a child, Sue. I'm not complaining about you being friends with her. It's just that when I asked you to pop round for a drink and a chat, you kept putting it off. I understand you've been through a lot. It's fine, really. So, are you going anywhere nice?"

"She's coming to me tomorrow night. We're going to have a couple of quiet drinks and some snacks to celebrate the lives of Eileen and George. And Amanda, of course."

"Didn't you do that at the wake?"

"Yes, but Tracy wants to do a private celebration. You know I'd invite you along, but that wouldn't go down very well, would it?"

Gina chuckled. "I could see the look on her face if I showed up."

"I'd have to shield everything," Sue said.

They both laughed.

"Well, you're going to feel very relaxed, I promise," Gina said.

"Only if you're up to it?" Sue said.

Gina nodded.

After Sue had left, she poured herself a martini and gulped it down, wondering if she was being used.

You should forget about her.

I'll have no one left.

She's using you.
We'll see next week.
You're really stupid.
What can I do about it, anyway?
End it once and for all!

***

The afternoon of Sue's massage soon arrived, and Gina had her table set up already. She'd only taken one sleeping pill the night before, to make sure she was up early enough. She had a shower, did her hair and looked more presentable than she had in days.

"That's better," Sue said, seeing her at the door. "The beautiful, glowing Gina is back."

Gina felt her cheeks go warm. "Stop it," she said, giggling. "I see you still have your smiley-face badge that I got you."

"Of course I do—I just haven't been wearing it lately," Sue said. "I want a full-body massage, with oil."

Gina went to the kitchen to get the oil, and Sue was already lying down when she came back into the living room. The candles were lit, and Gina put on soft music. She glanced at the yellow badge attached to Sue's cardigan hanging on the door handle.

CHAPTER-FORTY-SIX

Gina felt tired that evening, so she sat in her chair and closed her eyes, taking deep breaths to get herself relaxed. A certain loud voice was coming from next door; there was also laughter. Sue had told Gina they would have a couple of drinks to celebrate the lives of Eileen, George and Amanda.

Sounds like they're having more than a couple of drinks.

She put on the TV and her headphones—but she didn't fancy watching anything, so she found some ambient sounds. She closed her eyes again. The rain and the thunder in her ears, plus the dose of antidepressants she'd taken about an hour ago, soon made her feel more relaxed.

She was with Toby. They were running through an open field, side by side; Toby didn't even have his lead on, and there he was, running by her side. The thumping sound of the thunder in her ears was very deep, like someone hammering.

Gina opened her eyes. It didn't sound like thunder any more. She took off her headphones, confused for a moment. Someone was screaming her name.

She wasn't dreaming any more, she realised; someone was hammering on her door and window, screaming.

When she hurried to the door and flung it open, Sue was standing in front of her, shaking. Her white top and trousers had red splotches down the front, and her hands were covered in crimson stains.

Gina pulled Sue into the passage and held her arms. "What's happened?" she asked. "What on earth has happened?"

"I… I don't…" Sue violently shook her head. "Tracy's…"

Gina cupped Sue's face and made her look at her. "You need to take really deep breaths, Sue, in and out. Do it with me."

Gina took a deep breath in then out again. Sue eventually copied her, and Gina smelt alcohol on her breath, which didn't surprise her in the least.

But even after a few breathing exercises, Sue still couldn't get any proper words out.

"I need to go to your house and see, okay?" Gina had to force herself to take control of the situation, but her anxiety was all over the place. *So much for a relaxing evening.*

She took Sue into the living room and sat her down on the sofa. "You stay here. I won't be a minute."

Sue's front door was open. Gina crept inside and froze in the passageway.

Tracy was lying in front of the kitchen sink in a pool of blood. Gina moved closer, her hand clutched over her mouth. A large black-handled knife lay at an angle beside Tracy, covered in blood. Gina gently put two fingers on Tracy's wrist; she couldn't find a pulse.

Unable to stop herself being sick, Gina had to lean over Sue's sink. She splashed water over her face and swallowed a cupful of water in one. She glanced back down at Tracy.

She went back to her own house, where Sue was still shaking and crying.

"Sue, what the hell happened? What have you done?"

Sue didn't answer.

Gina picked up her phone.

Sue jumped up. "What are you doing?"

"I have to call an ambulance, Sue. Can't just leave her."

Sue dropped to her knees, and Gina helped her up.

"I'll support you every step of the way. You need to be strong, Sue."

It took the police just over ten minutes to arrive, along with an ambulance. Scene tape was put around Sue's house, and the village residents started to gather to see what was up.

Gina went outside. She stood watching from her garden, then she saw Carter's car pull up behind the marked police car. He talked to the uniformed officers, then went inside Sue's.

She went back inside to check on Sue, who had now calmed down just enough to talk in proper sentences.

"I'm going to prison, aren't I?"

"No. I'm sure there's an innocent explanation," Gina said. "Can you remember what happened?"

Sue paused, trying to think. She shook her head. "No, I can't remember. I remember we were talking about Eileen, and Tracy was telling me about some of the fun times they had. We'd drunk a bit too much, I think. Then… I don't know what happened. My mind's a blank."

Gina held Sue's hand when Carter walked in.

"Are you alright?" he asked. Gina nodded. "What happened here?"

"I don't know," Gina said.

Carter was looking at Sue, and the dried blood all over her clothes. He asked her again what had happened, and Gina squeezed her hand.

Sue just shook her head.

After five minutes of trying to get Sue to talk, Carter beckoned Gina to the kitchen. She followed him, and he leant against her kitchen table.

"Your friend is in a lot of trouble," he said. "I mean, we're talking murder here. She'll go to prison."

"Sue wouldn't kill anyone! There must be an explanation for all this. Maybe something was said and Tracy suddenly flipped and Sue had to defend herself."

"Inspector Kene won't see it that way. He thinks highly of Tracy Harper, as you know. I can't see a way out, I really can't."

"You can't send Sue to prison. She's harmless!"

"That's not what I'd call harmless. Have you seen the situation next door?"

Gina nodded. "I went in there. I couldn't get Sue to tell me."

"Well, whatever happened in there, she's got blood all over her. It doesn't look good."

A uniformed officer walked in and asked Carter to come outside. Gina went back to comfort Sue. She'd stopped crying; she had no more tears left. Gina sat beside her and held her hand.

"Miss Wilkinson!" That deep Scottish accent couldn't be mistaken. Kene and Gina stared at each other for a moment. "What's going on in this village? People are dying all over the place."

Gina shrugged. "How do you expect me to know?"

He looked at Sue, who had her head down. "What happened, Mrs Houldsworth?"

Sue didn't answer.

"I thought you and Mrs Harper were friends. If that's the way you treat your friends, then I hope you have no enemies."

"Leave her alone," Gina said. "Can't you see the state she's in? There's an innocent explanation—must've been self-defence. Something must've gone wrong, an argument broke out and it got so heated, Tracy must've gone into a rage. She can be very violent. I found that out."

"Well, it's a bit difficult to prove that, since the woman who could tell us what happened is lying *dead* right now!"

Gina took a step back. She'd never heard Kene raise his voice like that, not even when she slapped him.

Kene stormed out, and Gina sat back down next to Sue and put her arm around her.

"I can't go to prison," Sue said. "Who's going to take care of Mum? She needs me."

"Look, Sue. You need to say it was self-defence. You know Tracy has that violent temper—look how she reacted with me, when she thought I was after Colin. She pushed me against the door and punched me."

Carter came back, accompanied by a policewoman. "Mrs Houldsworth, please stand, turn around and put your hands behind your back."

"It was self-defence," Gina said.

"I'm sorry, Gina, but we have no choice. Stand up, please."

"It's going to be okay, Sue," Gina whispered, gently touching Sue's arm. "You have to be strong. I'm here for you all the way."

"Turn around and put your hands behind your back."

"You're not going to cuff her, are you? She's not going to do any harm—just look at her."

"It's procedure," Carter said. "Mrs Houldsworth, I'm arresting you on suspicion of murder. You do not have to say anything. But it may harm your defence if you do not mention when questioned something which you later rely on in court. Anything you do say may be given in evidence."

Gina could only watch helpless as Sue was handcuffed by the policewoman. Gina flung her arms around Sue; she could feel Sue shaking.

"M-my… My mum, what about…"

"I'll take care of it," Gina said. She put her hands on Sue's face. "Don't you worry, I'll see your mum's alright. You just be strong, and remember, it was self-defence."

She hugged Sue tight, but Carter gently pulled her away. "We have to go. Sorry."

Gina followed them outside. The other neighbours went silent.

"Don't look at anyone, Sue. Keep your head down," Gina said, remembering she'd done the same thing when she was taken on the night Annie Spencer was found in her garden, though she'd still felt all eyes were on her.

Gina watched the police car disappear up the road, then stopped on her way back in as the paramedics carried Tracy's body out of Sue's house. She felt nothing. At Tracy's place, there was a passage light on and a lamp shining in the living room. She didn't know where Colin was—he couldn't be at the village pub, because he would've been contacted by now—but she guessed he was away working; having a removal job, he often had to stay somewhere overnight.

Gina went back inside, sat down and took a deep breath. She thought about what Sue would be going through: being fingerprinted and having her photo taken, being led to an interview room or a cell.

There was a knock at the door. Gina didn't want to move, but she had to. Kene was standing there with a uniformed police officer.

"We need a statement about what happened, Miss Wilkinson. We need *everything*."

Gina told them everything she'd seen and heard. The officer wrote it all down, and then they left. Gina knew that Kene was in no mood to question her further; he seemed rather eager to get away from her, in fact, which suited her very well.

CHAPTER FORTY-SEVEN

That night, Gina couldn't sleep at all, so she got up just after 5 a.m., made a coffee and sat in her chair. Turning on the TV didn't help. She tried doing her colouring, but she couldn't concentrate on that either. The vision of Tracy lying on the floor, covered in blood, wouldn't leave her head, and she couldn't imagine what it was like for Sue in a holding cell at the police station. She just hoped Sue could get a decent lawyer and claim self-defence.

Later that morning, Gina called the police station and asked for Carter.

"How's Sue doing?" she asked.

There was a pause. "We had to sedate her last night. She's still resting right now."

"Does she have a lawyer?"

"We've allocated her one, yes. We hope to interview her this afternoon."

"Can I see her?"

"I'm afraid not," Carter said. "Not today, anyway—we're checking on some things. I'll contact you soon. We'll probably need to talk to you again."

Gina sighed. "When you do talk to her, can you let her know I contacted social services about her mum? They're going to pay her a visit. She might be able to have carers go in to check on her. Please tell her that."

"I will do, Gina. I have to go. Talk to you soon."

The phone went dead, and Gina glared at it. Carter hadn't seemed his normal self. For starters, he hadn't checked that she was okay; this irked her a little. He'd normally ask how she was, under any circumstance. She was a little surprised Sue had needed to be sedated, but at least she could rest calmly.

***

The next day, Gina was up early again. She'd slept a little better but had still been restless. She had some toast with her coffee, as she'd had practically nothing to eat yesterday, and she'd just sat down after a shower when her phone went off. Carter's name flashed up.

"Hello?"

"Could you come down to the station, please? We just need to clear some details with you."

"Can I see Sue?"

"That's up to the inspector. Tell you what, I'll come and collect you, save you a bus fare."

"Okay, great. I'll see you in a few minutes."

She went and got dressed, tidied her hair and waited for Carter. It took him just over five minutes to arrive.

Gina got in the front of his BMW. "How's Sue?"

"Not too good. We tried to interview her yesterday with her lawyer, but we didn't get much out of her."

"Did you give her my message about her mum?"

"Er, yes. I did. She seemed relieved by that."

The rest of the journey was quiet. Again, Carter didn't ask Gina how she was. He seemed a bit odd, almost like he'd gone cold on her.

They walked into the station, and Gina was told to wait in an interview room. This one was bigger than the others she'd been in. It also had a window, to her relief. She waited for about ten minutes, then Carter, carrying a laptop, came back with Kene. Carter placed the laptop on the table, along with a brown envelope.

Gina furrowed her brow at the items in front of her. "When can I see Sue?"

"All in good time, Miss Wilkinson." Kene gave her a smile which she didn't return and found uncomfortable.

"What's going on here? Why have you got a laptop in here?"

"You're helping us with our enquiries."

Gina looked at Carter, but his eyes darted away from her.

"Miss Wilkinson, do you recognise this item?" Kene pulled a clear plastic bag out of the brown envelope and placed it in front of her.

She was even more confused when she saw what was inside it.

"Yeah. It looks like the badge I bought for Sue." She stared at it again. The yellow smiley-face badge had a slight red stain on the edge.

Kene slowly took it out.

Gina's nerves were on edge—not because she was scared, but because the curiosity was overpowering.

"Just a normal smiley-face badge, right?" Kene said.

Gina nodded.

Kene got a thin black lead and plugged one end in the side of the badge and the other in the laptop.

"What kind of badge is this?" Gina said. She went to grab it, but Carter stopped her.

"I'd rather you didn't touch it, Miss Wilkinson. It's evidence," Kene said. He picked it up and held it in front of her. "Rub your finger over the right eye."

She did, and found the right eye had a slit across it.

"It's a camera. And it's fitted with a microphone. Obviously, you didn't know that, did you?"

Gina shook her head. "No, I didn't. I can't believe it! Clearly there's something on it you want me to see?"

"Yes. Let's have a look, shall we?"

Gina shrugged and nodded. Kene pressed some buttons on the laptop, and a video started to play.

CHAPTER FORTY-EIGHT

All Gina saw at first was a blurred hand, then Tracy came into view, holding an empty wine glass. She was in a white blouse and black trousers.

"Where did you get it from?" Tracy said.

"Gina got it for me in a charity shop," Sue said. Both their voices were slurred.

"Charity shop?"

"Yeah. I went with her to her doctor's appointment. It was my husband's anniversary, and she got it to cheer me up. Also, to mark our friendship."

Tracy rolled her eyes. "Cheap little tart could've done better than a charity shop."

Gina glanced at Kene and thought she saw a smirk on his face. She turned her attention back to the screen.

Sue was sitting opposite Tracy, who downed another glass of wine and was holding her stomach. "I think I'm going to be sick."

"Then get up to the toilet. I don't want sick all over my nice carpet!"

The screen showed Tracy hurrying past Sue, and there was a faint noise that sounded like stairs creaking.

Sue's grandfather clock chimed; it stopped at nine. Then there was movement on the camera; Sue was heading to the kitchen, and Gina saw her hand take a black-handled knife from the knife stand and lay it on the worktop.

Footsteps were heard coming down the stairs. Tracy came towards the camera, getting closer.

"That's better," she said, still slurring her words. "I need a hug, Sue." She stretched her arms out.

Gina saw Sue put one arm around Tracy's back, then she heard a sharp scream. Tracy backed away and looked down. Her hand started dripping with blood.

Sue pulled the knife out.

Tracy grabbed Sue's white top with her bloody hand. It was clear that she was trying to speak, but the words didn't come out; she just shook her head. There was a thump as she fell to the floor, blood pouring out of her stomach.

Tracy lay there gasping for breath. Blood spewed out of her mouth. She looked up at the screen and tried to speak, but only spat out blood.

The screen went blank.

Gina looked at Kene and then at Carter, who hadn't spoken.

"Was that self-defence, Miss Wilkinson?" Kene snapped.

Gina shook her head. "I don't know why she did it. Have you asked her?"

"She was too hysterical to tell us."

"Let me talk to her," Gina said. "I'm her best friend, I'm sure I can get her to—"

Kene held up his hand. "You can't talk to her."

"Why not? Just give me a few minutes."

"She's with the medic right now. And then she will be released without charge."

Gina looked puzzled. "But she killed Tracy! She committed murder! The evidence points to her. What about the knife? Her fingerprints must be on it!"

"You are correct, Miss Wilkinson," Kene said. "All will become clear in a few moments."

"You've had nothing on me this whole time," Gina said. "Are you saying you have something on me now?"

He turned the laptop towards himself so that Gina couldn't see the screen. After a few minutes of pressing buttons, he showed it to her once more.

She saw a still picture of herself in her living room and Sue lying on her massage table.

Gina stared at the screen. "Erm, what are you doing? You can't show this—it's private!"

Kene ignored her and pressed play.

Gina watched herself massaging Sue. She glanced at the smiley-face badge and slightly shook her head. "I don't know what you're expecting to find here."

"Let's see," Kene said, a slight smirk across his face.

CHAPTER FORTY-NINE

"Now that you're relaxed, Sue, you need to know what's really been going on around here. Let's start with Annie. That bitch kicked my beloved Toby. I was so incensed. She accused me of letting him go in her precious garden. He was only on the edge of her driveway. I so wanted to get revenge. I saw she was struggling with a bad back. So, about a week after our fight, I went up to her and apologised, saying I'd overreacted. It took some convincing, but she accepted my apology. I told her I'd massage her back for free, convinced her it would make it better. She accepted, and during the massage I got her so relaxed, talking softly to her. I told her she should jump out of her top window for kicking my dog. It was just a matter of brain power, getting her brain to tell her to do something. My ex-partner used to perform hypnosis on his patients. He showed me how to do it a few times; I must have picked it up well."

Gina sat there, shaking her head. She refused to believe what she was seeing and hearing. On screen, her mouth was moving and words were coming out, but it wasn't her talking. Her voice was sharp and aggressive.

"That isn't me. I don't know what's happening here, but I… I didn't." Gina started to shake. "I did apologise and offered to massage her back, yes, I admit that—but I don't remember telling her to jump out her window. Why would I say such a thing?"

"What about the hypnosis part, Miss Wilkinson?" Kene was staring at her so intently that she thought he was trying hypnosis on her.

"Well, yes, he did show me, and I took an interest in the subject. But I wouldn't use it. And anyway, you can't get someone to do something they wouldn't normally do. He told me that. I just can't remember saying all this stuff."

"It *was* you, Miss Wilkinson," Kene said. "All this sudden amnesia is just a smokescreen, an excuse to wriggle your way out of it." He stood and leant forward. "I know it was you, and that you knew what you were doing. And that's not all."

"I don't want to see any more. I want to go home."

"Well, you can't!" Kene started the video again.

"Oh yes. Jim Atkins. The guy that tried to rape me, Sue. Do you have any idea how disgusting he was? He thrust his hand down my underwear, putting his revolting lips on me. He was a bit drunk, but that's no excuse for what he did. I was desperate and scared. I told him I'd have sex with him as long as I could massage him first—you know, calm him down a bit. He accepted it, and I saw my opportunity. When I got him relaxed, my fear turned to relief. I told him after we'd finished, he would just go. I just wanted him gone. I thought I'd never see him again, but then he phoned me the next day, telling me he was sorry for the misunderstanding. He told me he was at the station, going to visit his parents, and he tried to book another session in for when he got back. I was scared and angry; I lowered the tone of my voice and told him to jump in front of a train. And believe me, Sue, I've done all women a favour."

There was no response from Sue.

"That's it—I've seen enough. Turn it—TURN IT OFF!" Gina jumped out of her seat, but Kene grabbed her arm.

"You're staying here till we're finished."

He continued the video.

"Then there was Amanda. What a complete bitch she turned out to be. I knew Tracy had put her up to it. She booked some sessions, then drew me in, pretending to be my friend, while all the time she planned to finish me off by planting drugs in my house and reporting it so I'd get raided. I couldn't prove it was her, but we both know it was." She slowly rubbed Sue's back.

Gina refused to look at the screen, so Kene turned up the volume.

"That bitch turned her back on me. I guess there was no real harm done, apart from the inconvenience of tidying up the mess, so I left it and carried on. Everything was pretty much fine for a while—they left me alone, and that's how I liked it. Little did I know the plans they were making, the plans to rip my world apart by taking my beloved Toby from me. I felt my life was done; my heart was ripped out of my chest. I didn't know what to do. The times when I thought about taking my own life, I saw Toby in my head. It was like him talking to me, telling me he was happy and to be strong, to get through this and come out the other end."

Gina was sobbing. She covered her ears, so Kene turned up the volume even more.

"Amanda came to me and asked for another session—only at her house this time. While I got her nice and relaxed, I thought about what she did, planting those drugs, pretending to be my friend. But she was *Tracy's* friend, she took orders from her, so I know she was involved with Toby's death. I told her to cut her wrists. She deserved it."

Again, Gina shook her head, refusing to believe what she was hearing, that it was really her saying all this stuff.

"The best is yet to come," Kene said.

He pointed to the screen, and Gina slowly turned to look.

"I don't remember saying all this stuff. I just don't remember!"

"Of course you don't, Miss Wilkinson." A smirk carved across Kene's face.

Gina watched herself rub Sue's lower back, working up to her shoulders. She didn't recognise the look on her own face. She dug a nail into Sue's shoulder blade, leaving a mark.

"Do you know what else really hurt me, Sue?"

There was no response.

"I not only lost Toby, but you turned against me as well. I thought we were friends, the best of friends. But I saw you with them, huddled outside together. You didn't come to see me, did you? And then when you were looking after your mother, I asked you if we could meet and catch up. You said you couldn't leave her. Only I found out that you *did* leave her and went out with those two bitches. How could I be so stupid? I realised you got me out of the house the day they killed Toby. It was your idea—you said it'd do me good to get out for a day. Only you didn't do it for me. You did it for that fat bitch next door; she's got you around her fat little finger just like the others. Oh, we need you to get Gina out of the house for us, you back-stabbing COW!" Sue continued to lie peacefully on the table as Gina moved slowly around her.

In the interview room, Gina thought she was going to be sick. "Water. I need water."

Kene paused the video. Carter got up and left the room.

"I don't remember saying any of this," she said. "I mean, I *felt* this stuff—I felt angry and hurt. Sue lied to me. I felt she betrayed me, my best friend! But I don't remember saying it."

Carter came back and handed her a plastic cup of water. She gulped it, spilling some down her chin.

Gina thought hard. Had she thought about or wished for their deaths so hard that she'd said it? Had she really brainwashed her neighbours without realising? Then Dr Southwell's voice entered her mind. *Temporary amnesia can happen, especially if you're really stressed or angry. The words just come out, beyond our control.*

"Not far to go now, Miss Wilkinson." Kene pressed the button to continue.

Gina saw herself grabbing a handful of Sue's hair. "It's okay, Sue, I made plans of my own. While you were having your fun, I went to see George. He was scared and reluctant at first, but he came around in the end. I knew he was a retired chemist, so he'd know about poison and stuff. He was scared of his wife. Eileen was the one who ran that household, just like her next door runs Colin's life. I find it sad, really. George knew what they'd planned. He overheard them—but he did tell me Eileen never spoke to him about it. But did he try to convince her what she was doing was wrong? Oh no. He just let her get on with it.

"They had a nice open fireplace. George told me he still chopped up the wood. That surprised me a little—he may have been seventy-five, but he clearly had plenty of strength left in his arms. So I told him to look at Eileen like she was a piece of wood for the fire. That took care of her. He must have panicked when he realised what he'd done. I didn't tell him to hang himself. I didn't want to hurt poor George, I was just angry."

Gina turned to Kene. "Please don't show me any more."

"I know, Miss Wilkinson," Kene said. "You don't remember telling Mr Levin to kill his wife with an axe, I suppose? After you brainwashed him, of course."

"I didn't go and see him. Well... I mean, I don't remember..." Gina put her head in her hands and sobbed hard. "I don't understand it."

"Almost there. You have to see everything."

"I'm going to be sick. I need the toilet—I need the toilet now!"

Kene tutted. He and Carter took Gina by her arms and led her to the toilets, where she spent ten minutes being sick and then splashed cold water on her face. She couldn't take any more. She was shaking so much, she had to get out. But they led her back to the interview room.

Back on the screen, she saw herself still slowly walking around Sue; then she crouched down to Sue's level.

"Why couldn't people just leave me alone, Sue? That's all I wanted—peace and quiet. Not even Karen left me alone when I was adopted, till my dad died. Even then, I didn't trust her. I happened to see her one night on my way back from a friend's house when I was eighteen. She was in an alley, having an argument with this guy—probably another one of her men. He pulled a knife on her. I backed off and made a noise, and he dropped the knife and ran. Karen was stoned out of her mind, so I picked up the knife with an old rag I found on the floor, and I stabbed her a dozen times. I watched her fall to the ground, bleeding. I remembered what she put me through and felt nothing but satisfaction. I then threw the knife in the river and went home. I wasn't questioned about it or anything. There was no blood on me—only the rag and my hands were covered in blood, and I threw the rag in a wheelie bin I passed. I got her out the way once and for all."

"I don't suppose you remember that either, do you?" Kene said.

"I remember seeing Karen after leaving my friend's house. She was totally drunk. I remember seeing this guy push her against the wall and pull a knife. I think I made a noise and he ran. My mind went blank."

Kene tutted. "Almost there, Miss Wilkinson."

Gina refused to look at the screen.

"There's one more person I need to deal with. It's like saving the best till last. Now, there's no way she's going to let me massage her, so I have to find another way." She grabbed a handful of Sue's hair. "That's where you come in. I'll teach you not to betray me." She let go of Sue. "You're having her over tonight, yes?"

Sue nodded slightly.

"This is what I want you to do."

Kene paused the video. "I've got to hand it to you, Miss Wilkinson—you're very clever. I never really believed in all that stuff, you know, unlike my wife." Kene chuckled. "She used to watch that guy on TV, Paul McKenna. She'd be in fits of laughter when he made people do crazy stuff. Drove me mad. I thought it was all fake, for entertainment purposes."

Gina stayed silent. She stared at the floor, feeling completely alone. She just wanted to be free, like her beloved Toby.

Kene picked up the smiley-face badge. "Imagine, you bought this for your best friend, not knowing it had a camera and a microphone fitted. Mrs Houldsworth must have fiddled with it and switched it to record without realising. If it hadn't been for this, you'd have completely got away with it all."

Kene pushed his chair back to get up. He towered over her. "You were the one who murdered Mrs Harper," he said. "It was you who plunged that knife into her!"

Gina lowered her head. She knew what he meant.

"Why couldn't they just leave me alone?" Gina said. "All I wanted was to live a quiet life, but no. All my life it's been the same." She fidgeted in her chair. "My childhood was ruined by Karen; she wouldn't leave me alone, even when I got officially adopted. People are so nasty and mean. This is Karen's fault. She messed around with other men, and one of them happened to be Tracy's dad, so she took it out on me." For the first time, Gina looked at Kene with kind, remorseful eyes. "I'm sorry I assaulted you. Sometimes I do stuff without knowing I'm doing it. I didn't want anyone to die! I didn't realise what I was doing. But what they did made me so angry! That, and the stress, must've made me do it. I was driven to it. Dr Southwell told me that can happen."

"I have no doubt you had murder in mind, Miss Wilkinson," Kene said. "And you learned hypnosis from your ex-partner, who was a psychiatrist?"

Sobbing, all she could do was nod.

CHAPTER FIFTY

Gina sat on the edge of her bed, staring out of the window. She didn't flinch when two people walked into her room.

"Gina?" the man said. "This is Alison. She's new here and will be looking after you."

She continued to stare out of the window.

"Hello, Gina," Alison said. "I'm looking forward to getting to know you." She was two inches shorter than Gina, with dark hair and round glasses.

"Gina's been with us for seven months now," the man said. "We had to place her on suicide watch; she's tried to take her own life several times. Twice she almost succeeded and had to be rushed to hospital. We now have a camera in here to make sure she doesn't harm herself."

"I read her report," Alison said. "I couldn't believe what I was reading, but I'm sure we'll get along fine."

"I'll leave you to get acquainted."

The man left the room, and Alison sat down next to Gina. "It's nice out there, isn't it? I like the fountain. We could sit out there some time if you want. Is there anything you like doing?"

Gina shrugged.

"I heard you like to do art stuff. We could do that too, if you wanted to. Or we can play some board games—you like board games?"

Gina nodded.

"We can get a group of us together."

"No!" Gina snapped. "No groups. I hate groups. I hate people."

"Okay, Gina," Alison said tentatively. "Well, I hope you can get to like me. We can have just us two play. However, I'd like you at some point to get involved with the others. We could introduce it slowly, over a period of time. I'm sure we are going to get along just fine."

Alison stood up, preparing to leave.

"Do you know why I'm here?" Gina said.

"Yes. I read your report."

Gina's eyes narrowed. "Then you'll know you need to keep me calm. Please don't upset me, like my neighbours. I would hate for anything to happen to you."

"Get some rest, Gina. I'll come by in a bit." Alison closed the door, leaving Gina on her own.

Gina never took her eyes off the door.

Do you have murder in mind? the voice in her head said.

"Only if she upsets me."

AUTHOR PROFILE

I didn't enjoy school one little bit. I struggled in nearly all subjects, however hard I tried. My favourite pastime was being at home watching F1 racing and movies on TV. I would rent out a film from the video shop practically every weekend, because I loved a good story. I didn't read many books until I was an adult, but then I became a constant reader.

I never imagined I would write a book of my own. However, one day this story came into my head and it wouldn't leave me alone. So although I had no formal qualifications, I thought: why not have a go? And now, eight years later, I'm proud to have achieved a fully completed published novel. I hope you enjoy reading it as much as I enjoyed writing it.

What Did You Think of *Murder in Mind*?

A big thank you for purchasing this book. It means a lot that you chose this book specifically from such a wide range on offer. I do hope you enjoyed it.

Book reviews are incredibly important for an author. All feedback helps them improve their writing for future projects and for developing this edition. If you are able to spare a few minutes to post a review on Amazon and Goodreads, that would be much appreciated.

Publisher Information

Rowanvale Books provides publishing services to independent authors, writers and poets all over the globe. We deliver a personal, honest and efficient service that allows authors to see their work published, while remaining in control of the process and retaining their creativity. By making publishing services available to authors in a cost-effective and ethical way, we at Rowanvale Books hope to ensure that the local, national and international community benefits from a steady stream of good quality literature.

For more information about us, our authors or our publications, please get in touch.

www.rowanvalebooks.com
info@rowanvalebooks.com